KV-370-976

# Torquere Press Novels

*911 by Chris Owen*
*An Agreement Among Gentlemen by Chris Owen*
*Bad Case of Loving You by Laney Cairo*
*Bus Stories and Other Tales by Sean Michael*
*Bareback by Chris Owen*
*The Broken Road by Sean Michael*
*Caged by Sean Michael*
*Catching a Second Wind by Sean Michael*
*Cowboy Up edited by Rob Knight*
*Deviations: Domination by Chris Owen and Jodi Payne*
*Deviations: Submission by Chris Owen and Jodi Payne*
*Don't Ask, Don't Tell by Sean Michael*
*Fireline by Tory Temple*
*His Beautiful Samurai by Sedonia Guillone*
*Historical Obsessions by Julia Talbot • Hyacinth Club by BA Tortuga*
*Jumping Into Things by Julia Talbot*
*Landing On Both Feet by Julia Talbot*
*Latigo by BA Tortuga • Locked and Loaded edited by SA Clements*
*The Long Road Home by BA Tortuga*
*Manners and Means by Julia Talbot • Music and Metal by Mike Shade*
*Natural Disaster by Chris Owen*
*Need by Sean Michael • On Fire by Drew Zachary*
*Old Town New by BA Tortuga*
*Out of the Closet by Sean Michael • Perfect by Julia Talbot*
*Perfect Ten: A Going for the Gold Novel by Sean Michael*
*Personal Best I: A Going for the Gold Novel by Sean Michael*
*Personal Best II: A Going for the Gold Novel by Sean Michael*
*Personal Leave by Sean Michael • A Private Hunger by Sean Michael*
*PsyCop: Partners by Jordon Castillo Price*
*Racing the Moon by BA Tortuga*
*Rain and Whiskey by BA Tortuga*
*Redemption's Ride by BA Tortuga*
*Riding Heartbreak Road by Kiernan Kelly*
*Roughhousing by Laura Baumbach*
*Secrets, Skin and Leather by Sean Michael*
*Shifting, Volumes I-III, edited by Rob Knight*
*Soul Mates: Bound by Blood by Jourdan Lane*
*Soul Mates: Deception by Jourdan Lane*
*Steam and Sunshine by BA Tortuga*
*Stress Relief by BA Tortuga • Taking a Leap by Julia Talbot*
*Tempering by Sean Michael • Three Day Passes by Sean Michael*
*Timeless Hunger by BA Tortuga*
*Tomb of the God King by Julia Talbot*
*Touching Evil by Rob Knight*
*Tripwire by Sean Michael*
*Tropical Depression by BA Tortuga*
*Under This Cowboy's Hat edited by Rob Knight*
*Where Flows the Water by Sean Michael • Windbrothers by Sean Michael*

This is a work of fiction. Names, characters, places, and incidents either are the product of the author's imagination or are used fictitiously. Any resemblance to actual events, locales, organizations, or persons, living or dead, is entirely coincidental and beyond the intent of either the author or the publisher.

A Private Hunger
SCREWDRIVER
An imprint of Torquere Press Publishers
PO Box 2545
Round Rock, TX 78680
Copyright © 2005 by Sean Michael
Cover illustration by SA Squires
Published with permission
ISBN: 1-934166-98-7, 978-1-934166-98-7
www.torquerepress.com
All rights reserved, which includes the right to reproduce this book or portions thereof in any form whatsoever except as provided by the U.S. Copyright Law. For information address Torquere Press. Inc., PO Box 2545, Round Rock, TX 78680.
First Torquere Press Printing: March 2007
Printed in the USA
If you purchased this book without a cover, you should be aware the this book is stolen property. It was reported as "unsold and destroyed" to the publisher, and neither the author nor the publisher has received any payment for this "stripped book".

# A Private Hunger

## Sean Michael

Torquere Press Inc.

romance for the rest of us

www.torquerepress.com

*A Private Hunger*

# Chapter 1

He grabbed the coffee cups off the table, whistling low and easy. His hips were still sore from last night's dancing, but it felt good, fine, a sweet burn.

Jennie popped his ass as she walked by. "You're too cheerful for words, Matt-baby. You get laid last night?"

Matt shook his head, red curls falling into his eyes. "Just dancing, Miss Thing. Just boogying."

She laughed and headed on, coffee pot held tight in her hand.

Two men came in together, one older, distinguished looking. Like a British butler really. The other was tall, striking, with hair like a mane, dark gold surrounding a golden face and falling down the man's back.

They sat at one of his tables.

Fucking hot.

He headed over, two menus in hand, telling his jumpy prick to behave. "Afternoon, guys. I'm Matt. Can I get you some coffee? Tea?"

"What about you?" asked the hot one.

Matt blinked, blushed dark and then recovered with a grin. Flirting. He could do flirting. "I'm working and not on the menu, sadly enough."

"I guess I shall have to settle for tea, then. I don't suppose you have something wild and strong?"

"We've got a nice blackberry and black tea." He craned his neck, looking at the specials board. "And another from South America that people seem to like."

The man growled, actually growled, looking discontentedly at his companion.

"I would be happy to drive you home and serve you what you want, Master Drakon."

The growling stopped, the hot guy's mouth twitching into a half smile. "I am most certain that you would not, Wetthers, though you are right, we have better teas at home."

'Master Drakon' turned back to him, and Matt realized that one of the man's eyes was brown, the other blue. "How much are they paying you to serve here?"

"Excuse me?" He blinked again. What an odd man.

The man's eyes narrowed and he asked the question again, enunciating each word very carefully. Matt noticed he had an accent, just barely there. "I asked you how much are they paying you to work here."

"I heard you, sir. I was just making sure I heard you right." Rude asshole. "I make minimum wage plus tips, same as every waiter in this town. Are you always this ill-mannered or am I just really lucky?"

To his surprise, the man laughed, the sound low and rich. "Oh, you are a feisty one. Go tell them you have been employed elsewhere and we will leave for my estate immediately. I shall double your salary and of course room and board shall be included. Wetthers will settle all the pesky details with you and the IRS as necessary."

Matt looked over at the old guy. "Is he for real? I mean, dude, you need a waiter at home?"

The old man seemed quite unperturbed by the goings on. "Master Drakon has made you an offer, young man. If you wish to accept it, I can assure you that it is 'for real'."

"Look, I'm not an idiot or a whore. You come in and tell me to quit my job and come with you without so much as sharing names, or you knowing more than I can walk and read a chalkboard." He shook his head, fingers moving to his side, his skin burning. "I'm flattered, but no, thank you."

The hot one -- Drakon -- growled again and then stood. "Well, if you change your mind and decide you want to know about the handprint on your ass, maybe I'll be willing to see you." Drakon patted his ass, but not right on, more to the side where his birthmark was. With that, the man walked out.

The man named Wetthers handed Matt a card with a stylized dragon on it and the words Drakon Estates. There was a number beneath it. "If you change your mind. Be very sure before you call."

"Right. Thanks." He watched the guy leave and shook his head. "Fucking weird. You see that, Jennie? That dude just propositioned me!"

"Weird." Jennie shook her head. "Glad he left before your shift was up. I hate waiting on ass-holes."

"Yeah." He nodded and pushed the card into his pocket. Real weird.

Guess he'd have to go dancing tonight to work

off the memory.

Whistling, he went back to doing his side work, mind filled with music.

*** 

Drakon was out hunting.

Quite unusual for him really, as it was day; he preferred to do his hunting under the moon's light.

Some odd twist of the stars or something had him out, though, restless and growly, belly rumbling, cock half-hard and rubbing against his leggings.

He wouldn't change yet, it took the fun out of the hunt, tipped the scales too far in his direction. Not that they weren't already tipped.

He let his instincts lead him deeper into the woods, moving further and further away from his Estate.

He moved closer to the road, scenting... something. Fear? Pain? Panic?

The trees opened to a clearing, and he found three people, one held still by the second while the third landed one blow after another. He growled. Well, that didn't seem quite fair. And on his grounds to boot.

He sprang into the clearing. "Unhand him."

"Unhand him? Look you fucking freak, whether this pansy ass gets beat or not ain't your business."

He growled again. It was personal now, and these two thugs were about to become dinner.

A knife came out, the beaten man slumping to the ground as he was dropped. Two men advanced upon him, sweating and angry, full of rage.

Oh, this was going to be fun. They wouldn't

taste the nicest, but the fight they'd put up should be more than worth it. He growled, fingers growing claws as he swung, taking the knife bearer across the chest and leaving four deep grooves.

"Jesus Christ!" The man screamed, taking a step back, shaking his head.

Drakon threw back his head and laughed. "He can't help you now."

Another swing caught the second man in the throat, leaving him to fall to the ground, bleeding out.

The first man turned to run, legs pumping as he tore into the trees. Drakon gave chase, letting the man think he had a chance before bringing him down with a deep bite to the back of the neck.

Drakon let the beast out, devouring this one whole before going back to finish off the other. The taste and smell of blood made him roar and feast, growling. They tasted sharp and stringy, but he'd had worse.

When the feeding frenzy eased, he heard the sounds of retching, the wounded man having crawled a few feet away.

He caged the beast once more, cleaning himself on the tattered remains of his shirt and approached the last man cautiously.

He recognized the red curls and long, thin nose, the bright yellow-green eyes, even swollen and bruised -- the boy from the coffee shop. His new pet.

Anger filled him, and if they had still been alive, or even just uneaten, he would have torn the two attackers to pieces. As it was, he had the satisfaction of having protected his own.

Bending, he picked the boy up. A soft sob filled

the air, the boy curling into his arms.

"It's okay, my Pet," he murmured, stroking the boy softly. "You're safe now."

He would bring his Pet home.

The soft, hot cheek rested against him, the trust instinctive, true. As it should be.

\*\*\*

Matthew ached when he woke up, room spinning, stomach roiling. It smelled strange -- smoky, old, wrong.

"Oh, God. Fuck." He rolled, groaning as the pain spiked.

"Sh, sh, sh. Stay still, Matthew. Wetthers is coming with something for the pain." The voice was low, almost growly, unfamiliar, yet it knew his name.

"Oh, please. Where am I? It hurts." He settled, moaning, eyes falling closed. Scared.

A cool cloth was placed on his head and long, warm fingers stroked his cheeks. "You're safe, Pet. No one will hurt you here."

"Safe..." He leaned into the touch, finding it an odd comfort. "The men... I was on my bicycle. They bumped me off the road..."

"They can't hurt you anymore, Matthew. Ah, here's Wetthers with your painkillers. Let me help you up." A strong arm went around his shoulders, lifting him into a sitting position.

The room spun and he blinked, trying to take in his surroundings. "I... Where am I?"

He opened his mouth and took the pills he was offered, moaning softly at the sweet, cool water.

"At Drakon Estates, sir." The kind face of the

old man from the coffee shop looked down at him.
"The Master is right. You are safe here."

"Oh. The... from work. With the pretty eyes.
The dragon man." He leaned back, relaxing into the
warmth that held him.

The man holding him purred. "That's right,
Matthew."

He smiled, or tried to, face tight. "Purring...
Tickles deep."

The long, warm fingers stroked his arms.
"Sweet boy."

He would have argued, but it felt good and he
was so tired, so stoned.

"You gave him too much, Wetthers," the low
voice growled, fingers stroking his face.

"No, Master Drakon; he is in a great deal of
pain. I have given him just what he needed. As he
heals, I will bring the dosage down."

Matthew moved into the touches, sighing, warm
with pleasure. It occurred to him that he should be
uncomfortable, that he shouldn't be cuddling with a
stranger.

Then it occurred to him that Drakon couldn't be
a stranger.

Not really.

"You are safe now, my Pet," crooned Drakon.
"Nothing can hurt you here. I will not allow it."

"Safe. Yes. Safe with my dragon." His words
confused him and he blinked. "I mean... I'm sorry.
Dizzy."

"Sh... easy, Matthew. No apologies, you are
fine. You are right. You are safe." The purring began again, Drakon rocking him slowly.

His body relaxed, finding a perfect, warm space
to sleep, to dream, to heal.

\*\*\*

It was a week since he'd rescued his Pet, and Drakon was getting restless. Wetthers had insisted on keeping the boy heavily drugged, threatening to take Matthew to the hospital otherwise. He had to admit, the boy had taken quite a beating, and he'd nearly changed his mind several times and taken him to the hospital anyway.

Drakon was loath, however, to let the boy out of his sight. So he'd agreed to let Wetthers keep the boy drugged hard enough to stay still and not feel the pain.

The bruises were fading now, though, and Drakon looked forward to being able to look into those amazing yellow-green eyes and see them clearly, not drug-glazed.

He spent the morning as he had every morning since Matthew had come to them, reading aloud to the boy. It didn't matter that Matthew was in a drug-induced sleep; it made him feel better to do it.

As the noon hour approached, he found himself dozing over his book.

He woke to the sound of the bed creaking, Matthew swaying in his boxer shorts, pale and thin, but awake, aware.

"Matthew," he murmured, standing at once and putting his arm around the boy, offering his support. "How are you feeling?"

"I... Better. Hungry. I need to pee." Those eyes blinked up at him, clearer now, like glass. "What day is it?"

He had to think for a moment. "Tuesday." He pointed and started leading the boy to the door next to the closet. "The bathroom is this way."

"Tuesday. Wow." Matthew shuffled beside him. "It's all very foggy -- the last few days, I mean."

"You were hurt quite badly, and the painkillers are very powerful. How are you feeling now? Any pain?"

"No. A little weak, not hurting." He got a grin, quick and clever. "I'm a little fuzzy on details, you know? A wee bit confused."

He nodded. "Let's get your bladder empty and you resettled. Then I shall call for Wetthers to bring you something light to eat, and you may ask anything you like so that we may sharpen your focus, yes?"

"Yeah. Thanks." The boy stopped suddenly, looking up at him. "I mean it. Thank you. You've been very good to me."

"You are most welcome, Pet."

"Matt." The boy moved into the bathroom, closing the door behind him.

He chuckled. Oh, he liked this one's spirit. "Call if you need assistance... Matt."

"Yeah. Thanks." It was a long few minutes before the door opened, Matt's face washed, unruly curls slicked back. "My face looks... Ew."

He chuckled. "Indeed. I'm not sure why the fine gentlemen who were beating you to quite the pulp thought you would look better so." He reached out, putting his arm around the boy's waist and taking a good amount of Matthew's weight.

"I don't think they were interested in my good looks, D." Matt leaned against him, a little frown between his eyebrows. "That's your name, right? D?"

"Drakon, actually. What were they interested in,

Matthew?" He asked the question casually as he
led Matthew back to the bed, *his* bed, helping the
boy climb up and settle against the mound of pillows.

"A pound of flesh and a hot hole, I think. Ass-
holes."

"They will not harm you again," he reassured
the boy. He tugged the old-fashioned bell-pull on
the wall at the head of the bed, calling for
Wetthers.

"Thanks for all your help. I would've been in
huge trouble otherwise." Matthew rubbed his head,
frowning. "God, I should probably call work, huh?
And the dude I'm rooming with."

"I believe Wetthers took care of that for you
when he fetched your gear here. We didn't think
you'd want to remain naked once you were on your
feet again." He tried to sound reassuring, but really,
he was hungry, the only thing holding him back
from pouncing on Matt was the discoloration in the
boy's face. He'd wait until any bruises that showed
were his own.

"You got my things? I... Oh, my driver's li-
cense, right?" The boy looked a little worried. "I...
is Michel going to hold my room for me? I'm not
due in Miami for another two months."

"I believe he made other arrangements. I'm
sorry -- I had no idea of your plans." He frowned
and then smiled, as if the idea just occurred to him.
"You could stay here until you have to go."

"I... I'm sorry, D. It's all a little fucked up and
weird right now. Maybe I could call my family, see
if they can come help. It's got to be bizarre, having
some stranger in your house." Matt's smile was
shy, cheeks flushed. "You've been so good to me. I

don't know how to thank you."

"You can thank me by not refusing my hospitality. You haven't been any trouble at all, really Matthew. Ah, Wetthers. Tell the boy he hasn't been any trouble."

Wetthers had a tray already prepared, some clear broth and a teacup, several crackers beside them. "No trouble at all, sir."

"Oh... The tea smells good." His Pet's stomach rumbled audibly, pale cheeks pinking.

He took the cup from the tray, offering it to the boy.

"You should try to get some of the broth down as well, Master Matthew."

"I'll try." Matt drank, moaning softly. "Oh, God. I was so thirsty. Thank you. Thank you."

Wetthers passed him the broth, giving him a look. "Get as much into him as you can before he falls asleep again."

"Thank you, Wetthers."

"If there isn't anything else?"

"Matthew?" he asked, giving the boy a soft smile.

"Hmm?" Matt blinked slowly, smile answering his. "Oh, no. No, thank you."

"Very good, sirs. Just ring, Master Matthew, should you need anything." With that Wetthers retreated, leaving him alone with the boy.

Matt finished about three-quarters of the tea, before setting the cup down. "Oh, that was perfect. Thank you."

"Will you have some broth? If you don't have at least a little, Wetthers will be quite cross with me."

That seemed to tickle his Pet, the laughter warm and bright. "I wouldn't want that. I'll have a little."

He dipped the spoon into the clear liquid and held it out to Matthew. After a little bit of awkwardness, Matt opened up to him, let him feed his Pet.

"I've never had anyone feed me like this." Another bite. "Not since I was a baby."

"Oh, I don't think you're a baby, Matthew."

"Good. I mean, I'm not. I'm usually not so foggy, either." Matthew took another bite, then finished the tea. "Honest."

He pushed Matthew's hair back, offering his Pet a warm smile. "I know, Matthew."

The dazed eyes blinked slowly, focusing up at him. "You... you have such warm hands."

"All the better to touch you with," he murmured, stroking the boy's cheek.

That got him a chuckle, green eyes drooping. "Mmm... the big bad wolf."

"Oh, I'm not a wolf, Pet." He mock shuddered. "All that pesky fur."

"No?" Matthew started giggling, pale cheeks pinking. "Good. I'm allergic to fur."

"No fur, I promise."

And hopefully, Matthew would not prove to be allergic to scales.

Slowly but surely, those unusual eyes closed, breath coming soft and easy, steady, sleep taking his Pet.

He stroked the boy's cheek again, fingers continuing down to the warm, soft skin of Matthew's neck.

His Pet was home.

\*\*\*

Matt woke up with a gasp, shaking from a nightmare filled with blood and claws and screams. He panted for a moment, then got out of bed, heading for the bathroom.

A shower.

A nice long shower.

Then he was going to put on some clothes and find a phone and call his folks. They had to be worried, had to be concerned.

A shadow moved out of the corner of his eyes and then his host was there, one hand taking his elbow. "Careful, Pet."

Pet? No. His name was Matt. "Had a bad dream. I need a shower. Made me sweat."

D frowned. "Are you sure you're up to that? I can help you."

"I want a real shower, D. A naked, no boxers, real shower." He grinned over, winking. "I'll bet I can manage." D wasn't *quite* enough of a nurse for him to be comfortable with the whole naked thing.

"I will wait here, then," D told him, giving him a smile that was just a little bit toothy in the darkness.

"'kay. Thanks." He shut the door behind him, stripping off his boxers and turning on the water. Steam filled the air, delicious and wet and...

He moaned as he stepped into the water.

Fuck, yes.

"Are you all right?" called his host. "Do you need assistance?"

"Hmm... Oh. Oh, no. Just feels so good." His voice sounded husky, rough.

"You're sure?"

"Mmm... Yeah." He lifted his face to the spray. "'m fine."

He froze as he thought he heard a growl, but it didn't sound again.

He soaped up, hands sliding over his skin, so slick, so soft. His cock filled, the heat and water feeling so good. Oh. Oh, yeah.

The door opened. "Pet?"

Matt jumped, slipped in the tub, hands reaching for the shower curtain as he started to fall.

He was sure he'd had it, but D was there, catching his naked ass and keeping him from doing himself further injury.

"Oh! You startled me!" He tried to regain his footing, hide his hard-on, get shit back to normal. "Sorry!"

"You must be careful, Pet, I would hate to see you injure yourself further." D's hands slid over him.

"I... Yeah." He found his feet, reaching for a towel to wrap around him. "I'm sorry. Thanks. Shit."

D hovered and fussed, finding another towel and wrapping it around his shoulders, patting at his wet hair with it.

Matt's cheeks were hot, body responsive and warm. "I... Thank you. You... Thank you."

"You're fevered," exclaimed D, picking him up suddenly and carrying him back to the bed. "I'll call Wetthers, get him to bring a tonic."

"Fevered? I don't feel..." He bounced on the bed, towels sliding free. "I'm okay. I promise."

"Nonsense, you were very badly beaten." D took the towels away and covered him with the blankets, tucking them around him.

"I'm fine now. Really." He settled back, relaxing, the bed familiar and comfortable. "You must be in the running for philanthropist of the year, D."

D laughed at that, the sound quite genuine. "Oh, Matthew, that was a good one. Philanthropist." D chuckled some more. "No, Matthew, I just like you."

"Me? Why? You don't know me, do you?" Christ, he was confused.

"I know enough, Pet."

Warm hands stroked his face. "You're tired, though, and still weak. Sleep, rest. Do not tax yourself."

His eyes closed automatically, the touch familiar now, soothing. "Need to call my folks. They'll be worried."

"I don't think that's a good idea."

Matthew frowned. "Why not?"

Mom would be frantic and Pop would... well, pretend not to be.

"It is the middle of the night, Matthew. Now, *I* believe that three a.m. is far more civilized a time than 3 p.m., but I understand that I am the exception to this. If you were to call your parents now, they would assume something was wrong. Which it isn't. Not really. You are safe here and mending well."

"Oh!" He blushed dark, giving D a sheepish grin. "Right. Stupid. My days and nights are all screwed up." Okay, that was embarrassing.

He was being petted again, D's hands sliding over his arm, his chest. "The lack of bright light from the window usually indicates night," teased his host.

His cheeks were going to catch on fire; he *knew* it. "Oh, right. Nighttime's when it's dark and stuff..."

"Yes, Pet. And stuff." And why did that sound so suggestive the way D said it?

"Why do you call me Pet? I'm not real small or fuzzy, you know." He shifted, hoping his cock would be quiet and still and limp.

D shrugged, hands still wandering over his skin, and that felt like more than petting now. Matt shivered, goose flesh rising -- and that was the *only* thing, damn it. "Aren't you sleepy?"

"I meant what I said about considering three a.m. more civilized. I do most of my sleeping during the day."

"I would do that, but I have to work. I take naps in the afternoon so I can go dancing."

"Dancing? I bet you look lovely." There was that suggestive tone again.

"I like to dance." He shook his head, feeling his curls bob. "No one with this hair is ever lovely. What do you do, D? To work at night, I mean."

D chuckled. "I'm old money, Pet. I don't have to work." Long fingers slid through his hair. "Quite lovely, really."

"Old money?" He lifted his chin, head rolling on his neck. He didn't let people touch him like this. "You've got to think I'm awful."

D returned to petting him, fingers on his cheek, stroking his belly, his thigh. "Because you have to work for a living? Why would I think that was awful?"

"No. I mean because I'm just letting you touch me like this. I just... it feels so good, so warm." God help him, his brain to mouth connection was fucking shorted out.

"I see nothing wrong with doing what feels good. Would you like me to hold you while you sleep?"

D was closer, already on the bed and gathering him to lie against the wide chest.

"Oh." He blinked, body relaxing almost immediately. "Oh."

D made a noise that he would swear was purring, holding him close, hand stroking along his arm in the most soothing manner.

It occurred to him suddenly that he was naked, but the touches weren't sexual, they were warm and easy, the touch of D's hand over his hip so good.

"You're safe, Matthew," murmured D, the words soft and reassuring, matching the easy touches.

"Mmm... 'kay." His cheek found a soft spot and he sighed, snuggling into his dragon.

No, Dra...Drakon. Into Drakon.

Maybe he was crazy, but he felt like he was home.

# Chapter 2

It was nearly dawn when Drakon came back from hunting.

He slipped into his room, watched his Pet sleep for a few minutes, and then went to shower, to clean himself up before Matthew could wake and see him. Matthew would soon be demanding his own bedroom, as was the boy's right, of course; he just... He enjoyed holding Matthew while he slept. Of course he would enjoy doing much more than just holding the boy, and he was eager for the days that he could come back from feeding and fuck until the need abated.

He growled, his need rising with his thoughts. He ached to take Matthew, to truly make the boy his own. However, happy, willing boys made better pets, pets that lasted longer. He'd learned that one the hard way.

So he took himself in hand, hissing at the sensation. Oh, he needed.

He thought he heard the mattress creak, the sound of his Pet shifting and sliding on the sheets. He could imagine the boy, the pale limbs shifting in the moonlight. He imagined that he was leaning over Matthew, lying on top of the sweet body as he fucked his Pet deeply. His hand was hardly a substitute for that tight body, but it would have to do. He squeezed harder, growling again, hips starting to move.

"D? D, are you in there? Are you okay?" The boy's voice was husky, rough with sleep and worry. "I thought I heard an animal growling..."

Oh mercy...

He cleared his throat, leaning against the tile, breathing heavily. "I'm fine." He cleared his throat and tried again. "Just fine."

"Oh. 'kay. Sorry. You... you mind if I pee? I won't flush."

He rolled his eyes. And then stood tall, pumping again. Let his Pet see his hunger. "As you wish."

"Thanks. Sorry, I couldn't wait." He could see the hint of the thin back through the curtain, see the dark smudge of a birthmark. His birthmark. He bit back his groan, hand moving faster. His. Matthew was his.

Matthew finished and turned, the line of that body delicious, disappearing out the bathroom door.

He did groan then, his beautiful Pet walking away from him. Oh, he wanted this one, didn't want to have to dispose of Matthew, not for a very long time. He saw the door stutter, imagined Matthew listening, still and curious, before the heavy oak was closed tight.

Soon. Soon he would be making love to his lovely Pet. Swallowing his roar, he came, heat shooting from his cock. He finished up quickly, eager to go see his Pet.

Matthew was sitting in the window box, cur-

tains open, the early sun pouring over him as he
meditated. The pale pajama pants were loose and
thin, the bottom of the birthmark still obvious, the
top section bare. He found himself growling, cock
growing hard again, and his silk robe was hardly a
good covering.

"That's the oddest sound. Who taught you to do
it?" Matt's eyes didn't open, body didn't tense.

"Taught me?" He growled again. No, he had
never been taught to do it; it was instinct. "My
mother, I guess. Perhaps my father."

Before I ate them.

Matthew chuckled. "Cool. My mom taught me
to sing some, but no growling. I need to call her
today, figure out what day it is and rent a car to get
to Miami. I don't know what I'd have done without
your help, D."

"Miami? Why would you want to go to Miami?" He felt panic crawl up his back, his cock
throbbing with his need to claim his Pet now.

"I've got a scholarship to study there. History. I
should have gone last September, but I've always
dreamed of the Pacific coast. Always. So I came to
spend a year." Matthew stretched up, shrugging. "I
love it, but I promised Mom I'd head to school after
a year of goofing off."

"Well, you still have a few weeks of goofing off
to do," he pointed out. "Why not spend it here? I've
quite the library that could be at your disposal."

"You sure you wouldn't mind? Just until August
15th, then I'll head out east." Matthew looked over
his shoulder, grinned. "I'm putting off moving
again."

"Not at all -- you've just moved here." He
smiled back. That gave him three weeks to win the

boy over before he had to force the issue.

"God, D. I don't know what I did to deserve meeting you, but thank you. I mean, I never could have afforded a hospital and stuff, and you've been..." Matt turned, one hand held out towards him. "Thank you."

He moved forward, taking his Pet's hand, and sat across from the boy on the window seat. "You let me rescue you -- made me feel all macho and important."

Those eyes were almost yellow in the sunlight, the boy flexible and relaxed with him, completely unafraid. "Yeah? Man, I was *not* feeling macho. I don't even remember it now, just little unreal flashes, the odd sound."

"It was not a fair fight. Only cowards and nasty little men gang up on others. I just evened out the odds." Thank goodness his Pet had been mostly unconscious. He had no intentions of hiding what he was, but there was no reason for it to come out too early.

"Did the cops come? I don't remember seeing any." His Pet blushed dark. "Of course, I mostly remember you. Weird, huh? I guess I knew who helped me."

"Yes, you did, Pet." He slid his hand along Matthew's cheek and pushed the curls back.

Matthew chuckled, eyes dancing at him, bright and playful. Utterly charming. "It's Matthew, D. and I know I need a haircut. I do."

"Matthew, right." He grinned back. His Pet would grow accustomed to his use of a... well, pet name. "Why not let your hair grow?"

"Mostly because my parents hate it. That and the guy I was... Er, my friend hated the curls." Oh, that blush was fine, too. Hot and dark, addictive.

"And what about you, Matthew? Do you not count?"

"Oh, I don't care about it one way or the other. Longer's easier, but shorter is neat and professional." He tilted his head, curls bobbing. "And less goofy."

"I think you look charming." He let his fingers run through the hair, caressing the soft curls. He wondered how they would feel wrapped around his shaft.

"Thank you." Those bright eyes closed, the look peaceful for a second before Matthew jerked and leaned back. "God, I'm sorry. You must think I have no self-control at all."

"Not at all, Matthew. I think you have considerable self-control. I am, after all, irresistible." He winked at Matthew, trying to gauge whether or not it was too early to take a kiss.

That got him a laugh, Matt relaxing. "Is it the hypnotic gaze or the incredible hands that do it?"

He pretended to be offended. "My unparalleled good looks!"

Another giggle, tickling and teasing. "You have great eyes. Nice hair, too. Must've taken forever to grow it out."

"Not as soft as yours, Pet," he pointed out, shaking it out over his shoulder and offering and handful to Matthew. *Touch me, Pet.*

Long, thin fingers took the mass, sliding over it, twisting it in the sunlight to see the colors. "Matt, D."

"Right." He gave Matthew a toothy grin, leaning close. He could smell the boy; oh, he could always smell Matthew, but up close he could pick up the more subtle musk of Matthew's body.

"It's beautiful -- golds and coppers. So pretty."

"It's hell to brush," he murmured, eyes on Matthew's lips.

"Is it? Do you need... I mean, do you have to get help with it?" That soft pink tongue slid out, wet that full bottom lip, leaving it glistening.

He breathed in deeply, the scent of Matthew's saliva arousing him further. "Are you offering to brush it for me, Matthew?"

"I... That's very... I mean, I haven't done it before, but I could." Those eyes -- so very green, so clear -- met his. "I could."

"I would like that very much... Matthew." He leaned in until he was close enough he could feel Matthew's breath against his skin, and then very slowly slid his tongue along Matthew's lower lip, picking up the sweet flavor.

"Oh." Matthew tilted his head, gave him a smile. "I liked that."

"Then I should do it again. Shall I?" He licked again, purring at the taste of his Pet.

Matt's tongue touched his, just barely, just enough to taste. He managed to swallow his growl, but could not keep himself from pushing forward, turning the touches of their tongues into a real kiss. Matt opened to the kiss, tongue sliding against his, hands holding his shoulders, keeping their bodies apart. He allowed his Pet that control, exploring the shape and flavor of Matthew's mouth. It wasn't long before he got a soft moan, the scent of pleasure and desire on the pale skin rich. He could not stop his growl now, not even if he had tried. Matthew tasted good, right. The boy was his, and their bodies knew it.

Matthew leaned back, lips parted, swollen. "That's a sexy noise, D."

"You bring it out in me, Pet."

Matthew shook his head, giggling. "Matthew, D. Or Matt."

"Will it get me another kiss?" he asked, willing to concede the point for more contact.

That got him a soft laugh, his Pet flirting. "Yes. One more."

"Very well. *Matthew*." He moved forward on the window seat, getting closer as he leaned in for his kiss. Matt was relaxed, happy -- Drakon could smell it on the pale skin, taste it upon those sweet, parted lips -- eager for his mouth, for contact. He explored Matthew's mouth again, and then enticed the boy's tongue back into his own mouth.

"Oh..." The soft gasp tickled his lips, and then Matthew tasted him, motions bold and sure, kissing him as surely as he had kissed. He growled gently, hands sliding up the boy's arms.

"Mmm..." Matthew shivered, scooting closer, tempted.

He slid his hands around to his Pet's back, encouraging the boy to move closer still, the low growl vibrating his chest continually. He needed. Oh, how he needed.

"So sexy. D. God, that growl." Matthew cuddled closer, thigh sliding against his.

He growled again. "For you, Matthew. For you."

"God... I should let you sleep..." He could smell Matt's arousal, Matt's need.

"I am not tired." He licked Matthew's lips and rubbed his nose along one cheek, hands sliding along the naked spine.

"No, but you're a temptation." Those hands began to move, stroking and sliding over the silk of his robe.

He growled again, pleasure doubling at the touches. "Matthew... " It was a plea and a warning. He would not be able to hold back from taking what was his much longer.

"Should I stop?"

"Only if *you* do not wish to continue. I want you, Matthew. Very much." He took one of Matthew's hands and brought it to his shaft. "Very much."

"Oh..." That hand started moving, sliding up and down, stroking him off. "I...I'm not a slut, D. I don't have any rubbers on me or anything."

A shudder moved through him, Matthew's hand warm and so good. It made it hard to think, made it hard to answer. Rubbers... oh! It hadn't even occurred to him.

"I shall send Wetthers out for some this morning," he murmured, eyes on Matthew's. "And I don't think you're a slut, Matthew."

"No? Good. Thank you. You're so hard, D, so hot." Matthew kept touching, his hand firm, warm, sure.

"How could I not be -- with you so close." He growled again, hips beginning to move with Matthew's motions.

"Flatterer." Matthew watched his eyes, the look fascinated, hungry.

He shook his head. "No, Matthew -- you make me ache for you."

"You have fascinating eyes."

He chuckled. Oh, what a delight, to have his Pet complimenting his eyes as the boy's hand drove him slowly mad. "Thank you," he managed, finding breath to give sound to the words.

"Mmm... just truth." Matthew leaned forward and licked the corner of his mouth.

He moaned, turning his face, searching for a kiss. Matthew gave it to him, tongue pressing deep, hand working his shaft faster and faster. He growled, hands moving randomly over Matthew's skin, all his attempts at seduction set aside in favor of the sensations going through him. His passion flared, drawn through him by soft hands, soft lips. He found Matthew's waistband and slid his hand into the loose pajama bottoms, Matthew's hot flesh jumping into his hand, bringing another growl from him.

"Oh! Oh, D..." Matt pushed closer, whimpering, kiss deepening. "God..." He drew the boy into his lap, hand tightening, pulling on the hard cock he held, pushing into Matthew's touches. "D!" His Pet arched, shuddering hard. "Please!"

His free hand wrapped around Matthew's neck, tilting the boy's head just so as his kiss devoured his Pet's mouth. Growls filled him, filled his Pet's mouth, his hands and hips moving together.

Matthew whimpered, heat splashing over his hand, teaching him the scent of his Pet's need. He let himself go, let that scent push him over. Pleasure spilled from him. Matt leaned forward, panting. "Oh... Oh, God."

He chuckled, the sound husky, sated. "No Matthew, it's Drakon. Or D."

Matthew's laughter tickled his throat, hot and happy. He purred, bringing his hand up to his mouth and tasting his Pet from his fingers. Oh, yes. This scent and flavor were forever imprinted on his

brain now. He would be able to find Matthew anywhere.

"So sexy." Matthew moaned, settling against
him.

He growled quietly, pleased. His hands slid
around his Pet, holding the boy close, safe within
his arms. Matthew was his now. It was only a matter of time before his Pet realized it for himself.

***

"I'm okay, Mom. Honest." Matt rubbed his
head, watching the sun set.

"Are you sure?" His mother's voice was worried, low. "You're going to make it to Florida on
time, won't you?"

"Yeah. Yeah. I need to rent a car and I'll head
out in a few weeks." He stretched, scratching his
belly, listening as she rambled and fretted and lec-
tured. Parents.

D wandered into the drawing room, looking
rumpled yet handsome, hair unkempt, silk robe
adding credence to the thought that D had just gotten out of bed. The man smiled when he caught
sight of Matthew, moving slowly toward him, eyes
gleaming.

Matt offered D a warm, happy smile. "Mom.
Mom, I'm fine. I am. I'll be in Miami as promised,
'kay? I need to go. Love you. Bye."

He hung up the phone with a soft laugh. "My
hero! She can talk my ears off."

D came up to him and slid his hair back on both
sides, fingers warm and soft along his ears.
"They're still there, Pet."

He laughed, face lifting for a kiss. "Good to

know."

D gave him one of those sexy little growls and then took his mouth, tongue sliding deep, fingers holding his face. He moaned into D's lips, shivering and arching close, tongues meeting. God, so sexy. D's arms wrapped around him, pulling him tight against the long body, the kiss deepening, becoming hungry.

The passion flared, so hot, so *big*. Matt gasped, pulling back a bit, trying to clear his head. "I can't think when you do that."

"What do you need to think about, Pet? I want you. You want me. It is simple." D's mouth slid over his jaw, his neck, teeth scraping now and then, D's hot tongue following, soothing.

"I need to think about my plans, about contacting my friends, about..." His head fell back. "Oh... Oh... what was I saying?"

"Something about not thinking," murmured D, lips and tongue and teeth slowly working their way back up to his mouth.

"Oh, okay." He wound his arms around D's neck. Electric. This man was electric and caring and willing and passionate, and the best way to spend three weeks he'd ever met.

Ever.

D kissed him like the man was going to devour him, all need and hunger and heat. Panting and hot, he held on tight, moaning into D's mouth, rubbing against that strength.

"I want you," growled D.

"You just had me... what? Yesterday? In the window?"

"No, Pet, that was a little mutual pleasuring. This morning I want to bend you over my bed and take you." D's voice was little more than a hungry growl.

"Did you get the rubbers?" He'd done that before -- not a lot, but a few times, yeah.

"Yes. Well, technically Wetthers got them." D winked at him. "But they're in my side table drawer."

"I just left your bed, and now you're inviting me back for a visit?" He gave D another kiss, still stunned that the dear man had given up his own bed for him.

"Indeed, I am." D's hands slid along his back, cupping his ass, squeezing.

He moaned and nodded. "Okay. Okay, but I'm not... I'm not like a real stud. I've only had one real lover, you know?" Just in case it wasn't *completely* obvious. God, he could be a dork. Good thing it wasn't perpetual.

"If I wanted a stud, I'd be at the Downs, checking out the horseflesh. You'll do just fine as you are, Pet." D gave him another dizzy-making kiss.

He stepped closer, moaning. "Oh. Oh, good."

D gathered him up into the strong arms, one beneath his shoulders, the other beneath his knees, and began to carry him up the broad staircase, peppering his face with hard little kisses.

"Wow. You... Strong. You're strong." He hoped to hell that Wetthers guy didn't show up right then. It would be *embarrassing*. D gave him a pleased growl. The man wasn't even breathing heavy by the time they got to the familiar room with the big bed. He licked D's jaw. "Love that growl. Never heard anything like that before."

"Yeah?" D growled again for him, longer, lower, the sound vibrating the broad chest against him as he was set down on the bed.

"Yeah." It made him hard, made him want. Made him a little scared, too, just a little, just enough to make him shiver.

That made D growl more, the hot mouth closing over his, stealing his breath as equally hot hands slid beneath his t-shirt. His skin burned, ached, and he shifted, not sure if he was trying to get more or get away. D pushed his t-shirt up, their kiss breaking to pull it over his head. He blushed a little, arms ending over his head. "I spend a lot of time half-dressed around here."

"Oh, that won't do," murmured D. "It won't do at all." D pulled at his sweats, sliding them down off his legs. "There, now you aren't half-dressed anymore."

He laughed, turning halfway to playfully hide himself, showing D a long line of skin.

D growled again, pouncing on him, mouth slick and hot along his side. "Such sweet skin, Pet." He could feel those hot fingers tracing his birthmark, tongue soon following the same path.

"Mmm... Oh! Sensitive! God, D!" He moved away, goose flesh rising. "Oh, that's... that's something else.."

"It is beautiful." D slid his hand along the birthmark.

"My mom wants me to get it removed, says it'll get cancer, but I never have." It was an ugly blotch, almost like a handprint. Almost.

D snorted. "It is quite beautiful, Pet. There's no need to remove it."

"It tingles when you touch it." There must be some weirdness with the nerves. Odd.

"A good tingle?" D asked, fingers stroking,

tongue licking.

"I... Yes. I mean, not bad. Diff... different." His knees buckled, eyes rolling back into his head. "Wow."

D growled again, the sound sliding along the mark.

"You... you'll make me come." He whispered the words, embarrassed but *so* aroused.

"You say that like it's a bad thing." D didn't stop.

"But... I... Oh, D. It feels good..." He stretched out, hands on the bed as his body rippled.

"So beautiful, writhing for me." D traced the birthmark with his tongue, fingers dancing over it. "Come, Pet, and then I will have you."

"Matt. Oh, D... Oh..." His hips jerked and then D growled again, teeth sliding against his skin, and he came, shooting hard.

D rolled him, licking his prick, cleaning him. He moaned, almost whimpering, little shocks sliding over his skin. His cock, his belly, his balls, they were all licked long past the point of being cleaned, D just exploring. Matt was shivering, lost in those touches, hands sliding through that thick, dark hair. D's growl sounded again, as his legs were spread apart, that licking tongue sliding behind his balls.

"Oh!" That felt... Oh, God. He sat up, crying out. "That's... I mean... Oh. You. You surprised me."

No one had *ever* tried that before.

D looked up at him, strange eyes so hot. "I was tasting you, Pet. Lie back down so I can do it properly." D's hands pushed at him.

He leaned back, shaking. "That's... that's so much, D."

A Private Hunger

"This?" murmured D. "This is just the beginning, Pet." Before he could even figure out what D meant, that tongue was back, sliding along the crease in his ass. The sensation was huge, and he arched, fingers fisting in the sheets, thighs parting. D growled. "Taste good, Pet."

Then D began to lap at his hole, tongue pressing just the littlest bit in.

"D..." He sobbed, shifting. "Oh... Oh, God."

Then D pushed that hot tongue right in. Oh, God, he was hard. Hard. Fuck. Babbling, too. Never felt this. Not with Billy, not with Adam. Never. Oh, God. Oh, fuck. Please. Over and over D fucked him with that tongue. Then all of a sudden D stopped, pawing through the side table drawer, growling as he came up with a condom.

He drew his knees up, nodding. "Oh... Yes. I want you."

D nodded, getting the condom on quickly and then kneeling between his legs. "Beautiful, Pet," D growled. He could feel the thick heat of D's cock against him.

"Oh... It's... You're big, D." He tried to relax, belly rippling.

D leaned forward, licking at his lips. "Big and strong and yours."

His mouth was taken, D's tongue invading as D's prick started to spread him. It burned. Deep and hot and undeniable. He cried out, eyes meeting D's in a mixture of desire and panic. D growled into his mouth, fingers sliding over his birthmark. The tingle made him jerk, made him cry out, made him arch onto that stiff heat. D's growls changed tenors, grew deeper, hungrier as D sank all the way in. He couldn't move, couldn't think, couldn't do much more than pant, focus captured by tongue and cock.

D began to move, fucking him slowly, heat moving inside him. He shifted, shoulders lifting as he started meeting the thrusts, starting moving and sliding. D's growls grew stronger; the thrusts into him grew stronger. He reached down, grabbed his cock and started tugging, crying out into D's lips. The growl became something closer to a roar, D fucking him harder, faster.

Fuck, yes.

He screamed, jerking hard, dancing on that prick, come splashing over his belly. D threw his head back and roared, cock pulsing inside him. The shudders rocked him, breath trying to slow. Fuck. Sex had never been like this. Never. Oh, wow.

D pulled out and got rid of the condom before lying down next to him, nuzzling along his jaw line. "Thank you, Pet."

"Matt." He chuckled and grinned, a little giddy.

D growled. "Matt."

Matt leaned over, giving D a kiss. "Yeah."

D blinked at him sleepily and then kissed him back.

He settled into the pillows. Maybe a nap. Then a walk or something. Find the kitchen. See if they had any tofu dogs. Or hummus.

Mmm... hummus...

D's arm pulled him close to the warm body, staying against his hip, curling around the birthmark.

He cuddled in, happy with the world.

# Chapter 3

Drakon woke up hungry.

For three days, he and Matthew had feasted on each other's bodies, making love over and over.

Now he needed to feed, to fill his belly.

He slipped from the bed. Matthew moaned, shifting, reaching for him even in sleep. He reached back, hand sliding along the birthmark.

His stomach rumbled, reminding him that he had to feed.

Sleepy yellow-green eyes cracked open. "You okay, D?"

"Just going to get a bite to eat, Pet." He stroked the boy's cheek.

"Mmm... I made some tabbouleh. 's in the fridge." Matthew moaned softly, eyes closing.

A vegetarian. His Pet was a vegetarian. The universe did have a sense of humor.

"Thank you, Pet." His fingers were kissed and then Matthew was asleep again, snoring quietly, pale and lovely on his bed.

He watched for a moment longer and then went to feed. Matthew needed to sleep, for he would be hungry for his Pet after he'd eaten.

Several hours later, just before dawn, he returned to his room. He didn't even look at Matthew, knowing he needed to take a shower, wash away the blood and stench of the hunt before going to his Pet. One day he would not have to, but his instincts said it was too soon to let Matthew know his true nature.

He was clean, the hot water pouring over him when the shape of his Pet moved beyond the shower curtain, using the facilities, a husky, still-sleepy "mornin' D" sounding. He growled, need pushing to the fore.

He managed to wait until Matthew was done and then leaned out and grabbed his Pet's arm, pulling Matthew into the shower.

"Want you."

Matthew blinked, stumbling close against him. "You're real awake."

"I am," he agreed, pushing Matthew up against the wall, plastering his body against his Pet's.

He took that sweet mouth, devouring it, so hungry for mating now that he'd fed. Matt squeaked at the cold tile, cuddling into his arms, still not completely awake, lax and loose in his arms. Those lips parted easily, letting his tongue in, letting him have what he needed.

One of his teeth nicked the soft skin on the inside of Matt's bottom lip and he growled, sucking, pulling the taste into himself. He rubbed against Matthew, his shaft hard and hot and needy, dripping heat that mixed with the water.

Matthew moaned, hands tangling in his hair. "Easy, D. Shit, easy. I'm not going anywhere. Relax."

"Need you," he growled, hands sliding back and grabbing Matthew's sweet ass.

"Hungry." Matt's legs wrapped around his

waist, the weight comfortable in his hands.

He growled happily. "Starving for you, Pet. Absolutely starving." His cock rubbed against Matthew's ass and he used his fingers to spread the boy's cheeks wide.

"Need to get a condom, D. The lube. You won't fit." Matt's lips found his throat, licking and sucking.

He growled, annoyed, wanting. Needing. Those lips slid over his skin, up to the hollow beneath his ear, a soft moan sounding. His instincts warred, on the one hand he needed to take Matt, on the other he didn't want to frighten the boy.

Snarling, he dropped Matt back to his feet and turned off the water. He grabbed his Pet's hand and dragged him to the bed, both of them still dripping.

Matthew was shivering, a little frown on the pale face. "You okay, D?"

"Need," he managed, pushing Matthew onto the bed.

He grabbed a condom and the tube of lube from the side table. Tossing the tube at Matthew, he growled, "Now."

He tore open the condom wrapper, spreading the latex over his shaft, growling, almost shaking.

When he looked over at his Pet, at the slick fingers disappearing into that tight body, hot cheeks hidden in the pillows, his growl became a roar. He climbed onto the bed, biting at the birthmark on Matthew's skin before licking at Matthew's fingers, at where they disappeared into the tight hole. He could taste his Pet beneath the oily flavor of the lube.

"D... Oh, fuck." Matthew shivered, the ring of muscles clenching around those fingers as a sweet moan sounded.

"Yes. Now." He used his mouth to pull Matthew's fingers from his body, licking the fingers clean before surging up and pressing into his Pet.

The sweet body arched for him, the low cry of pleasure dripping with need. Matt's curls bobbed as they moved, his Pet hungry for him too, riding his cock. He bit at Matthew's skin, peppering his Pet's shoulders and neck with small marks as he thrust, sinking again and again into glorious heat.

Words filled the air, nonsense cries and pleas -- a sweet song that his Pet sang to their need. Harder and harder he pushed, need overwhelming everything. His growls got louder and louder, until he roared, coming hard.

When the red haze cleared, Matt rested, warm and damp and relaxed beneath him. "Oh. Wow."

He growled softly, licking at the myriad bite-marks on Matthew's shoulders, hand stroking his Pet's belly. Soft shivers met his caresses, Matt's seed slick against his fingers.

He moaned as he pulled away from the tight grasp of his Pet's body. He got rid of the condom, growling slightly; he couldn't wait to be rid of the stupid things -- it wouldn't be right until he could sink into his Pet's beautiful body without any barriers.

Trembling fingers grabbed a tissue and wiped off the thin belly, then Matt was pushing into his arms. "Gonna go back to sleep, now? I'll make some muffins or something later."

He kissed his Pet. "Yes, Pet. Sleep. We're safe here."

Matthew nodded, pulling the blankets over them and snuggling close. Soft eyelashes tickled his skin as those sweet eyes closed.

He threw his arm and leg over his Pet. His.
Even if Matthew didn't know it yet.

\*\*\*

Three weeks since he'd been run off the road
and he'd never once left this big old house.

He hadn't really had to -- Wetthers bought
whatever groceries he asked for, there was a
swimming pool, a vast library, and then there was
D.

Damn.

He'd never thought sex could be like that. Wild
and hot and...

Wow.

Still, it was well into August. Time to start
packing. Time to go. Time to leave.

He scooped up a bite of hummus on a cracker,
munching, watching D drink a glass of wine. "Will
you come and see me, do you think?"

D froze and very carefully put down his wine.
"You're going, then?"

"I have a scholarship." He sighed. "I promised
my folks I wouldn't do this -- wouldn't come here
and get involved and then not want to go."

"You're willing to let go of me just like that,
Pet?" D looked very unhappy.

He put down his bowl, moving around the table,
drawn to his lover. "I don't want to go. I don't. But
I have to go to school and stuff."

"Couldn't you... I don't know -- using a computer or something? I keep hearing about remote
schooling." Poor D wasn't the most technically in-
clined man.

"I wish. I mean, you can once you've started, but I haven't." He settled in D's lap. "I wish I already had the stupid degree and could just find a good job here and stay. You... you're special, D." His heart was breaking, but he'd made commitments, promises. He was good at keeping his promises.

D growled, not looking any happier. "You don't need a job to stay here. My home is yours, Pet, just as I am."

"I can't just bum off you forever." Matthew petted the soft, thick hair, held his lover.

"Why on earth not?"

"Because... uh... because it's not fair to you and I'm supposed to make my own way and stuff." He hated when D asked weird questions.

D snorted. "What utter rot." Warm, strong arms wrapped around him, pulling him close against the solid body. "I want you to stay, Matthew."

"I want to stay, too. I do." He whispered the words, eyes filling with tears. "I made a promise, D. I promised I wouldn't come down here and fall in love."

"But that promise is already broken, Pet. Going wouldn't change that."

He blinked hard, meeting D's eyes. "You knew already? How I felt about you?"

"If you weren't in love with me, you'd not be letting me talk you out of going." He got a toothy smile.

"I... D..." He couldn't help smiling back. "Stop it. Stop making me want to stay right here forever. It's not fair."

"No -- what isn't fair is you leaving. I don't want you to go. You don't want to go. Stay." The last word was growled, D's hands hard on his hips, pulling him in even tighter. Leaning forward, D nibbled at his neck. "Stay."

"Oh..." He lifted his chin, shook. "Oh, D..."

He couldn't stay. He... Oh, God help him, he wanted to stay.

D's fingers worked his clothes off, pulling away his t-shirt and making short work of his jeans. One hand wrapped around his prick, thumb sliding across the tip on the upstroke. "Stay."

"That's cheating. What if Wetthers comes in? What if... Oh..." He arched and gasped. "More, please."

D growled softly, hand continuing to stroke, mouth sliding over his collarbone.

"You're... you're seducing me. You..." He stopped fighting, hands tangling in D's hair, hips rocking up into the touches.

D didn't answer him, just kept pulling on his cock, free hand sliding back to cup his ass, long fingers holding hard.

He pushed into a kiss, shaking and close, drowning in the wildness of his lover. D's mouth devoured him, hand hard and insistent on his cock.

He shot hard, crying out into D's lips over and over.

Oh, he was so fucked.

D growled and licked his come from that large hand. Those strange eyes were so hot.

"Do you know how sexy that is? How... sensual?" He took another kiss, feeling all melty.

"I only know that I crave your taste." D's tongue slid over his lips and pushed in briefly. "My turn, Matthew. I want you."

"Mmm... Yes. Yes, D." He nodded, working

open D's shirt to touch the strong chest, the peaked nipples.

D growled that sexy growl for him, hips pushing up, letting him feel the need trapped by D's pants.

He scooted down, unfastened the cord that held the soft pants up. On. Whatever. When he got D's prick out, he leaned forward for a long lick up one side, then rubbed his cheek down the other side to leave a kiss on the soft balls.

"Oh, Pet..." D growled, hands sliding through his hair, fingers massaging.

He licked and nibbled his way back up, moaning at the sensation, at the flavor. He wasn't very good at sucking D off, not yet, but he was getting better.

"Yes..." D's hips arched up toward his mouth, fingers stroking his scalp, silently encouraging.

His tongue explored the ridge around the tip, the slit. His fingers cupped the so-soft balls. The whole time he moaned, breathing hard. Wanting.

"More," growled D.

He pushed his tongue a little deeper, wrapped his lips around the head of D's cock and sucked. D's hips jerked, his lover roaring. The hands in his hair tightened and needy growls filled the air. His eyes closed and he relaxed, just sort of floating and sucking and tasting.

The growls were like caresses, settling in his belly and his balls. It made everything hotter, those noises, and he moved faster, sucked harder.

"Pet..." The growls got louder, slid toward roars, warning him that D would be coming soon. Matthew cupped D's balls, rolling him almost roughly.

A long roar filled the air, D shooting hard. He swallowed what he could, some escaping from the corner of his mouth.

D's finger wiped the come from his chin. That wicked tongue lapping it away. "Not nearly as sweet as you, my Pet."

"D..." He blushed, rubbed his face on D's belly.

D rumbled, skin vibrating beneath his cheek. "So. No more talk of leaving?"

"I have to call my folks, the school." Matt sighed. "If we're lucky, they'll just yell over the phone and Mom won't show up at the front door. She'd scare even you."

"Don't give her the address," D told him.

"D! She's my Mom!"

"Yes. And aren't mothers-in-law notoriously evil? I have no wish to have her show up and scare me, Pet." D's fingers were sliding over his skin, finding his birthmark and tracing it.

Mother-in-law. Oh. Oh.

Matthew settled back up in D's lap. "You have a point there."

"I have many points," D told him, winking.

He chuckled. "You do. Good thing I like them."

"Yes," D agreed, seeming suddenly very serious. "It is."

Lifting his head, he met D's eyes, watching the blue and brown until his head was spinning, his heart pounding, birthmark on fire. "Yours."

Heat flared in those eyes, a low growl starting. "Yes." D's mouth covered his, hard and toothy, hungry and taking. He opened wide, pushing back, wanting so badly. Loving. Needing.

"Let me take you," growled D. "Just you. No plastic."

He nodded before he let himself worry. If this was going to be long-term, he was going to have to trust D, trust him with everything. D's growl was triumphant and hungry, needy. His lover's hot mouth began to move over his skin, nipping and licking at his neck and moving down from there.

His fingers were tangled in D's hair, spine arched. "D..."

"Taste so good, Pet."

His nipples were both licked, bitten. D's teeth scraped along his breastbone and nipped at his navel. D's hands were his only support as he was bent further and further back.

"Don't let me fall, D." He stretched, his body trusting where his mind couldn't.

"Never," growled D, mouth surrounding his cock, teeth sliding along the skin, just enough to notice.

He pushed up, moaning, muscles growing tight. D nibbled at his cock, licked and worried his skin, but didn't linger, kept moving down, forcing his back further and further over the strong hands. His hands found D's legs, used them for balance, for stability, for focus.

D growled. "Wrap your legs around my neck, Pet."

It took a second, but he managed, head spinning.

"Perfect." D dove in, licking at his balls, at the skin beyond, teasing his hole.

He cried out, not caring if Wetthers heard, if the whole world heard. He simply needed. D growled at the sound of his cry and began to stab into him with that hot tongue. Matthew's heart stopped, entire world shrinking to the wet heat of that tongue.

Then the growling began again, vibrating inside him through D's tongue.

Oh, fuck. He was going to come. He was. Oh, shit. Oh, God. "D! D, please!"

D just kept growling, kept tongue-fucking him. Then one hand raked across his birthmark, finger-nails scratching. He shot hard, eyes rolling up in his head, room going grey.

When he came to, he was bent over the divan, D biting a line down his spine, hot cock nudging at his hole.

"Mm... D. So hot." He stretched out, hips tilt-ing.

D growled and pushed into him, filling him slowly, cock hot and hard and like silk covered steel.

Oh... He spread farther, moaning. "D... I can feel you!"

"Yes."

D stopped moving once he was all the way in, fingernails slowly sliding down his back. He was lost in the sensation, sobbing, whole.

"So hot. So tight. My Pet." D started to move, cock hard and insistent, sliding against his gland again and again.

"Oh. Oh, God." He panted, cock trying to fill, trying to get hard again.

"No, Pet. Drakon. Or D." The words were rather breathless and growly and then D stopped talking and kept fucking and it was unbelievably hot and good.

His body shuddered, slowly going from needy to desperate, body burning. D's hands settled on his hips, pulling him back onto each thrust. He was going to die, going to dissolve, going to fucking melt.

D's hand wrapped around his cock, tugging in time with the thrusts that were getting harder, coming faster.

"Y...yours! Yours!" He arched, screamed, thighs shaking.

"Mine!" The word was roared, D shoving into him hard and then he could feel the heat of D's come shooting deep inside him.

The sensation sent him flying, seed pulsing from him, something deep inside easing.

D's hand left his cock and he could hear the sound of his lover licking at his come. Soft, slow strokes slid along his spine and then with a groan, D slid from his body.

Matthew whimpered, eyes closing. He was going to die right here. Sleep forever on this couch.

D picked him up. Or, he could die in the strong arms, that would work, too.

\*\*\*

Well, that had been close.

He really liked Matthew, and it would have been a shame to have to eat the boy.

Now he just had to worry about the mother.

He curled up around his Pet, nuzzling as Matthew made I'm awake and getting up noises.

"Do you have to tell them you're not at school?" he asked.

"Hmm?" Bleary yellow-green eyes focused on him, blinking slowly. "Well, what else would I tell them? Eventually somebody's going to want to come visit me, D. My brother, folks, somebody."

"Sure, of course, but they don't have to know

right away do they?" It would be better if the subject of visitors didn't come up until Matt knew his true nature, knew how dangerous it could be to have a curious mother poking through his things.

"No... but I don't want to lie to them." Matt's eyebrows lowered, a crease on his forehead. "It's bad enough I'm breaking my word. Lying's like adding insult to injury. They love me, D. They'll be mad, but they'll come around. I just have to find another school. There's Northwest near here. Heritage. I can apply for the winter. That will keep me here and satisfy them."

The winter. That would give him time, he could live with that. Better yet, so could his Pet.

"Tell them to blame me, Pet. Tell them I can't live without you and won't let you go."

"Oh, yeah. Right. Can't live without me." Matt gave him a grin. "I don't even know how old you are, what your full name is. When your birthday is. All I know is that you've got pretty eyes and are irresistible."

"I'm older than I look, my full name is unpronounceable and my birthday is May the 1st. Sexual favors are my preferred gifts." He winked at Matthew and slid his hand down along the boy's side to his hip. "How about we test the irresistible thing now?"

"May 1? Cool! Mine's December 21st." Matthew chuckled, moving easily under his hand, chin raised for a kiss. "Hungry man."

"Always hungry, Pet." He pressed their lips together, tongue invading the sweet mouth and picking up the flavors of his Pet.

His Pet nuzzled, hands sliding over his belly, his hips, his balls. He growled, pushing into the touches as his own hands slid over Matthew's skin. He was being petted, hair and spine stroked in long, slow motions.

Arching, he purred for Matthew.

"Oh, you like that." Matthew rolled him over and started massaging his spine, petting and touching and caressing him without hesitation, without fear.

He arched and purred and fisted his hands into the sheets. If Matthew didn't stop, his Pet would whip him into a frenzy of lust. Fingers found one bundle of nerves after another, soft kisses trailing behind. His prick grew hard and harder still, excitement settling in the base of his spine.

"Pet," he growled, warningly.

"Matt." He was goosed, Matthew's chuckles sliding over his spine.

He growled again, flipping and putting Matthew beneath him, devouring his Pet's mouth with his own. When Matthew had gone breathless beneath him, he ended the kiss.

"Matt."

"Huh?" Matt blinked up, utterly confused.

He laughed, pushing his need against Matthew, once again devouring the boy's mouth. Matt wrapped around him, arms and legs holding him tight. Such a treasure, this one. His mouth slid along Matthew's jaw, down to the fine neck where he began to bring up marks.

His treasure.

Matthew moaned, chin lifting. "Oh... that feels... D..."

"Mine," he growled, working up another mark. His hips were moving, the urge to sink into his Pet strong.

"Mmm..." The moan was needy, rich. Wanton. "D."

"Mine," he repeated.

He made a grab for the lube on the side-table, knocking it onto the floor in his impatience. Matthew twisted, mouth fastening on his shoulder and pulling hard. He growled, spreading Matthew's legs and rubbing his dripping shaft along the hot skin hidden there.

Hot and soft, his Pet's body jerked against him, seeming to tempt him in. He whimpered, wanting so badly, needing. He nudged forward, testing. Still stretched from their earlier encounter, Matthew accepted him with only a soft hiss, lips parted as his Pet arched.

He growled, pleasure and need slamming through him. His. Matthew was his.

He bit at Matthew's skin, teeth breaking the skin. The flavor of Matthew's blood suffused him, sinking into him. A cry split the air, Matt rippling around him, body jerking.

He began to thrust wildly, overcome with lust and need, sucking at Matthew's blood. Matthew was clutching at him, cries meeting each thrust, trembling in his arms.

"Mine," he roared, pushing harder, so close.

"Y...yes. Yours. Yours." The scent of seed filled the air, come and blood.

He roared, coming hard enough to see stars.

His Pet curled in his arms, shaking, moaning softly. He stayed buried inside the sweet body, hands stroking, mouth kissing. He hadn't been this taken with anyone in decades.

Possibly centuries.

A soft kiss brushed his shoulder, green eyes

dazed, trembling fingers moving to pet his hair.

"My sweet Matthew," he said softly, nuzzling into the touches.

"Mm-hmm. Yours." His Pet relaxed for him, eased with the weight of his purrs.

Yes. His.

# Chapter 4

It was funny, even with D keeping him up later, Matt never could manage to sleep all day, especially now that summer was loosening its grip, the wind a bit stronger, a little cooler.

He'd taken his bike out around noon, heading out to the city. He checked his box -- four furious letters from mom, a naked chick postcard from his brother, a few bills, nothing major. Then he bounced in for lunch at the coffee shop, bought two new shirts and some hummus with the last of his savings, then pawned his violin.

He hadn't quite figured out the whole asking for money deal. This kept man thing was... challenging.

Matt rubbed his neck, wincing as his fingers scraped over a wound. Hell on the skin, too.

When he came out of the store, Wetthers was waiting for him. "You do realize I would be more than happy to run errands for you, Master Matthew?"

"Wetthers! Damn! Do you have a magical radar homing device implanted on my butt?" He offered the old dude a smile. "I needed to check my mail and buy some winter shirts. I'm betting the house gets drafty. Do you know if we have apple juice at home?"

"It is on my list to buy, sir. You do remember that you need only tell me what you desire and I will make sure to stock it?"

"I..." He held up the bag with his few groceries. "It's just tough to get used to, you know? How long have you worked for D anyway? You know so much about him."

"I have worked for Drakon Estates since I was a boy, sir."

"Wow. So you knew D's folks? Wicked!" Matthew grinned. "You'll have to tell me baby-D stories one day."

Wetthers didn't reply, but the look on his face was a very genteel and understated version of 'no way in hell, sir'.

"Spoilsport." He winked. "Are you still running errands or heading home?"

"I would be most happy to give you a lift back to the Estate, Master Matthew."

"Yeah? Cool. Thanks." He walked his bike over to the big old car, and stashed it in the huge trunk.

Wetthers frowned at him as he went to sit in the passenger seat.

"What? Did I do something?"

"You should sit in the back, sir."

"Oh. Are you picking D up?" He opened the back door and got in. Christ, he'd lived in *apartments* smaller than this car.

"No, sir."

Wetthers started the car as soon as he was in, the ride smooth and luxurious. He settled in, watching the scenery, half dozing. It looked like a storm was blowing in, the first real hint of fall. It seemed no time at all before they were pulling up along the wide drive.

"If you'd like to go right in, sir, I can take care of your things."

"I can put my bike up. No sweat." He grabbed his shirts and stuff from the backseat and hauled his bike out of the trunk, stowing it in the garage. "I'm going to see if D's awake and hungry. I have fresh hummus. Maybe he'll try some. Stubborn man. Bye, Wetthers!"

Wetthers' "I wouldn't imagine he will," followed him into the house.

He put the food in the kitchen, his shirts in the room that D had given him, and then went looking for his lover in the big bed. The curtains were drawn and there was a lump in the middle of the bed, deep snores confirming it was D.

He nearly tripped over the man's clothes on the floor. "Tsk, tsk, Wetthers, that's not like you."

He picked them up to put on the chair, only to discover they were tattered and covered in blood.

"Fuck! D! Drakon!" He hurried to the bed, heart pounding. Oh, fuck. Somebody broke in and hurt D. Fuck. Fuck. "D! Wake up! Where are you hurt?"

D surged up, covers flying an almost inhuman snarl coming from the man.

Matthew stumbled backward, falling hard on his ass with a cry. "D! Drakon, it's okay. I won't hurt you. Shit. Wetthers! Help! He's hurt!"

D crouched on the bed a moment and then leapt toward him, arms coming around him, big body surrounding him.

Wetthers was there a moment later, calm as always. "What seems to be the trouble, sirs?"

"He's hurt. There's blood everywhere." Matt

could smell it, feel it all sticky and gross, and he was trying not to move or hurl or anything that would make it worse.

D growled again, the sound a bit calmer, the arms around him loosening.

"Oh, I don't believe Master Drakon is hurt, Master Matthew." Wetthers went around to where he'd dropped the clothes, picking them up quite calmly.

"Pet? You're not hurt?"

"Me? Me? No. No, D. *You're* the one that's hurt." He blinked over at Wetthers, completely wigged. "Aren't you worried? Don't you care?"

One of Wetthers eyebrows went up. "Are you hurt, Master Drakon?"

"No," growled D, hands moving over him now, checking... checking to make sure *he* was okay.

"Stop it!" He grabbed D's hands, careful not to squeeze. "I'm fine, please. Listen to me. There's blood everywhere, D. Who *hurt* you?"

"No one hurt me."

"Perhaps, Master Drakon, it is time to tell him." D growled, nodded.

"I shall fetch the whiskey."

D nodded again and waved Wetthers away.

"Tell me what?" He stood up and took a step back, frowning. Shit that started like this was never good. Never.

"You better go sit," D told him, pointing to the bed.

"It's dirty." He backed away and settled in the window seat, watching D closely, trying to ignore the panic gnawing at him.

D stayed in the middle of the room. "I am more than I appear."

"Whose blood is it, D?" His voice was pretty smooth, considering.

"My dinner's."

"Wh....what did you have for dinner?" His hands were cold, his feet, too. The back of his neck, though, was hot.

"I am not a vegetarian, Matthew."

A soft knock sounded on the door, Wetthers coming in unbidden. A glass with pale liquid was pressed into his hands. The decanter and another glass on a silver tray were placed on the dresser.

"Call if you need me, sirs." With that, Wetthers left them alone again, drawing the door closed behind him.

"No. I knew that. I *know* that. Why is there blood, D?" He looked down into the glass, it was the color of hay. He took a sip, shuddering at the burn.

"Do you believe in dragons, Pet?"

"Dragons?" Okay, this was weirder than average weird. "Like big flying, fire-breathing lizards in D&D?"

"Not quite as fantastic as all that, Pet, but that is the general idea, yes."

He took another sip, trying to warm himself. "I... dragons? Are you trying to tell me you ate a dragon?"

God, D needed help. Real help.

Real serious psychotherapy-type help.

His mom was going to love this.

"No, Matthew, I am not trying to tell you that I ate a dragon. I am trying to tell you that I *am* a dragon."

"A dragon." Maybe psychotherapy wasn't strong enough. That sounded deep and serious,

lock-you-away-type crazy. Like 'maybe you
shouldn't be in the room alone with D, Matt' crazy.

"You know it's true, Pet. In your heart."

He shook his head. "D. You... you need some
help. People aren't dragons. What did you eat? I
mean, undercooked beef is *nasty* with germs, and
there's a lot of blood." He took another drink, not
looking. He couldn't help D if he was puking.

"I wasn't eating beef. Believe it or not, Pet, I
agree that it is nasty -- even fresh on the hoof."

"Please. Please, Drakon. You're scaring me."
He shook his head, trying to clear it. "Let's get you
to a hospital, see if they can help you."

D walked slowly toward him, sitting next to
him on the window seat, those mismatched eyes
holding his the entire time.

D raised a hand, gentle fingers sliding over his
cheek. "I'm fine, Pet. Just fine. And you're safe
here."

His eyes filled with tears, head shaking, automatically nuzzling into the touch. "D... I don't want
you to hurt, but there's so much blood. What bleeds
like this?"

The room was getting dim, the sun sinking.
Night time coming.

"Your attackers did," Drakon answered him
softly, hand still stroking, soothing.

"Hmm?" He shook his head again. "What do
you mean? You mean... No. You can't mean that.
God, you can't."

"You know the answer to that, Pet. You have
from the start. You were there when I rescued
you."

"I don't remember any of that." He didn't. He
didn't. He just remembered D holding him after.

D slid those warm, wonderful arms around him, drawing him against the wide chest. "It's all right, Pet. Nothing's changed. You're still safe here."

"Nothing... Nothing's changed? You promise?" Tears were sliding down his cheeks and he didn't cry, he *didn't*, but he couldn't stop, couldn't help falling into D's arms.

"I promise." D growled, the sound low, rumbling, as soothing as the arms that held him tight.

D handed him his glass and he finished the last few mouthfuls, head cradled in D's chest. "I didn't want you hurt. You scared me."

"Sh... you didn't hurt me, Matthew, you couldn't."

D began to rock him gently, those soothing purring noises vibrating against him. "We were all a little startled."

His eyelids drooped, so heavy, so relaxed in his lover's arms. "Yeah. You should eat hummus. It's not as messy as... this."

"If I could, I would, sweet Pet." A soft kiss landed on his head. "But ewwww -- hummus."

Matt started giggling, the sound welling up from deep inside him.

D growled softly. "I'm not going to have to slap you, am I?"

He hiccupped, giggles trailing off. "No. No, don't."

D kissed him softly. "Why don't you rest, Pet? When you wake you can ask me the two thousand questions I'm sure you have."

"I..." He sighed, nodded. "I'm tired, I guess. I mean. Yeah." He was tired, head swimmy and foggy and blah.

D kissed him again. "Come sleep with me. The

bed is lonely without you."

Matthew hesitated. There was a reason he didn't want to get in the bed. A reason.

There *was*.

But he couldn't remember why and he didn't care why anymore. He just wanted his D.

D drew him into those strong arms and rocked him slowly. Matt closed his eyes and hid, let D protect him, let D hold him.

Everything else was just details.

*** 

Drakon let Wetthers change the sheets on the bed and set the room back to rights before moving to the bed with Matthew. The boy slept deeply in his arms, knowing instinctively that he was safe. Well, he supposed he had to credit it in part to Wetthers' concoction.

He thought it hadn't gone too badly. Matthew was, after all, still with him.

Of course he wasn't convinced that Matthew actually believed him. Humans had such fantastic imaginations, and yet time and again refused to believe anything that was outside of their realm of experience. It was one of their biggest failings.

He nuzzled into Matthew's neck, nibbling at the sweet-salty skin. He was always horny after feeding, and he hated having to be patient and wait.

Matt whimpered, pushing towards him, legs curling up towards the thin chest.

He stroked his Pet, hand sliding over smooth skin, glad that he'd let Wetthers help him undress Matt. It hadn't been easy, though; his instincts had been to protect and defend, even from Wetthers himself. Anyone else would have lost a limb, just for being in the room.

His hand came to rest on the dark patch on Matt's hip -- proof that Matthew was *his* -- and his Pet shivered, the mark hot against his palm. He stroked it, fingers sliding over it. He could feel the tingles in his own fingertips. The exact shape of his hand, each of his pets had been born with it, been born with his need, his mark branded into their flesh.

As far as he knew, they weren't related, it wasn't some family trait passed down from generation to generation. Indeed, there had been times when he'd gone hundreds of years between pets. Which made him all the more careful not to drive them away.

Fingers and claws, scratched deep into pale flesh, and this one felt *good* next to him, around him, against him. Matthew felt right.

He started nipping at Matthew's collarbone, taking mouthfuls and letting his teeth graze the warm skin. His Pet started moaning, shivering, head falling back to offer him that sweet throat.

The need rose in him, and he growled, pushing Matthew onto his back, biting hard enough now to leave lurid marks. Matthew cried out, eyelids fluttering, hands opening and closing on his shoulders. He licked the marks he left, nuzzled them, smelling his Pet's blood, drawn close to the surface by his lips and teeth and tongue.

Matthew eased, relaxing with a soft moan, hands sliding down his spine. "D..."

He growled softly, nipping at one sweet nipple, making it go dark.

The flesh hardened against his tongue, wrinkling and tightening. "Mmm... 's good. Good, D."

His hands slid along Matthew's flesh, pulling Matthew closer, letting his Pet feel the heat of his need. Pliant and fluid, almost purring himself, Matthew undulated, body sliding along Drakon's strength.

So responsive, so right. He growled again, and bit at Matthew's lips. "Mine."

"Yours. So hungry, my dra..." Matt's words trailed off, a frown creasing the high forehead.

"Always hungry for you, my Pet." He nuzzled Matthew's forehead, cheek rubbing against the lines, trying to smooth them out.

"Love you, D. I... Mmm... feels so good." Warm open lips slid over his skin, tongue licking softly.

He purred and pressed closer, hands pulling Matthew tight against him.

"Mmm..." Matthew's shivers felt delicious against his skin.

He dragged his fingernails down along Matthew's back, from shoulders to buttocks. Matt's spine bowed, body arching up toward him, yellow-green eyes going wide. He growled, hands grabbing the sweet ass, sliding their cocks together, watching his Pet's face, watching those beautiful eyes.

He was watched, devoured by them, those eyes wide and focused and clinging to him almost like a touch. He growled, passion flaring higher at Matthew's obvious pleasure in him.

He began to take biting kisses. The heat between them grew, flared, turned into sheer need. He bit his way down Matthew's body, licking and tasting and taking what was his.

His Pet was hot, hard, clear liquid sliding along

the thin stomach. He lapped it all up, took the source into his mouth, sucking hard; Matthew tasted sharp and sweet and salty all at once. Thin hips started jerking towards his mouth, pushing quick and hard, Matt's cock throbbing and hot.

He sucked a moment longer and then lightly bit his way down the hot flesh, threatening the drawn up balls with the same treatment. Thin legs raised, Matt's body instinctively trying to avoid his teeth.

He chuckled and kept moving, using his hands to spread his Pet's legs far apart so he could lap at the little hole.

"D! I... Oh, I need! D!" Matthew writhed, sobbing desperately.

He growled, blowing against Matthew's hole before licking, taking in the dark musky flavor. His Pet keened for him, muscles going taut, ring of muscles convulsing beneath his tongue.

"So sweet." He licked and teased, slowly wetting the hot little hole.

The limbs under his hands started rocking, finding a rhythm and pressing towards his tongue. He rewarded his Pet's eagerness by pointing his tongue and pressing it inside. Matt's body gripped him, squeezing his tongue in time with the breathy cries that filled the air.

He humped the sheets, worked his tongue faster, needing to take his Pet -- he would not be able to hold back much longer.

"D! D, please! Please, I *need*!" The words slammed into him, rich and passionate, hungry.

"Then you shall have," he growled, moving quickly to lie between his Pet's legs. "Open to me, Pet, take me in."

"Yes. Yes, D." His Pet bore down, impaling that

fine body on his cock, enclosing him in a hot, tight grip.

His growl bordered on a roar, Matthew taking him in was so good.

Slowly, steadily, Matt fucked himself, taking in more and more until ass and hips were snugged tight together, rocking. He would have let Matthew fuck himself until they both came, but his own need and hunger were too great and with a growl, he shifted, pushing Matthew's legs further back with his arms and fucking his Pet hard.

It didn't take long before his Pet screamed, seed spraying, body convulsing around his cock. Bending he bit into Matthew's shoulder, pulling several drops of his Pet's lifeblood into himself as he came, too.

Matthew's arms wrapped around him, held him as he relaxed, petted him. Finally Matt gave a trembling sigh and whispered. "Are you going to kill me? Why did you bring me here, D? Why didn't you kill me out there?"

He growled, unhappy that Matthew had doubts about his place. "You are safe with me, Pet. You are *mine*. I brought you here so that we might please each other."

He slid out of his lover and turned Matthew over. "You see this?" he said, hand sliding over Matthew's birthmark. "Look how it fits my hand perfectly."

"I..." Matthew frowned. "How? How did you know?"

He shrugged. "I just did. Call it instinct, if you must."

"You're a murderer, right? That's what you were trying to tell me before." Those eyes were still, calm, completely focused.

He frowned. "I don't believe it is murder, Matthew. I need to eat. I kill to eat. Men hunt animals all the time and do not call it murder."

"You eat other people? Oh, D... D, that's gross." Matt shook his head, shivered. "The police are going to lock you up when they catch you. You'll get the electric chair. Can't you stop?"

He chuckled. "No, Pet, I cannot stop." He kissed Matthew's forehead, thankful for Wetthers' concoctions. Eventually Matthew would come to accept it. He didn't know if his Pet was ready to do so on his own yet. "And I haven't been caught yet. I don't plan to be."

"How long? Ten years? Five? How often does it happen? Do you hurt them?" Now that the questions started, they flowed out in a deluge.

"How long? Oh, Pet... I'm far older than I appear to be. And it happens as often as I am hungry. I usually kill cleanly." Except when killing men who dared to mess with his Pet, though he didn't say it aloud.

"This whole thing makes my head hurt, D." Matthew curled in close, nuzzling his chest. "I... Stay with me?"

"Then don't think about it, Pet. I would not have you hurting for anything." He put his arms and one of his legs around Matthew, holding him close. "And of course I will stay."

A soft whimper sounded, Matt's arm sliding around his waist. "Thank you."

"You're welcome, Pet," he murmured, kissing Matthew's forehead.

The boy was warm and solid against him.

So good.

It had been far too long since he had had one of his own to keep.

\*\*\*

He'd slept and slept. When he dreamed, D was there, giving him a drink, holding him, whispering to him.

Safe. He was safe. Here. Here with D.

His D.

His.

His big, growling, purring dragon.

Dragon.

Oh, God.

Matthew took himself to the bathroom, water from the shower pounding down on him as he sat in the tub and tried not to think. Dragons weren't real. They weren't. They couldn't be.

Drakon, though.

Drakon was real.

Oh, God.

The door opened. "Pet?"

Speak of the devil.

"You should have woken me -- I would have joined you earlier."

"I... I needed to get clean. I've slept forever." He shuddered, so undone.

One of D's growls sounded. "I can help you get clean."

"Yeah? You think? Promise?" He wasn't sure. He felt... icky.

Drained.

A little lost.

D got into the shower behind him, standing close and pulling him up against the hot, solid body. "Always, Pet."

He melted into the strong arms -- he wasn't sure he wanted to, but he knew he needed to. "Mmm... so hot."

D purred for him, the sound soothing and vibrating along his back. The strong hands moved over him, slowly spreading soap. Matt let his eyes close, let D touch him and ease him and love him, his own soft sound answering his lover. He was washed and then turned this way and that in the stream of water, soap rinsed free.

"I love when you touch me, D. Feels good." Matthew felt sort of like a rag doll, limp and loose-limbed.

D purred, hands continuing to move on him. No part of him was left untouched.

A thousand questions slammed into him, but he couldn't find the will to ask them. For now, this was enough, this lethargy, this peaceful need.

D's purrs deepened, the large hands slowing, moving minutely, gently.

"Is it magic? This between us?" He raised his face for a kiss.

D's mouth closed over his, tongue softly tasting. "I do not know, Pet. I just know it feels good."

"It does. Oh..." He met D's eyes, taking another kiss and another. "Bed. Take me to your bed."

"As you wish, Pet." D picked him up and cradled him against the powerful chest, stopping only long enough to grab a towel for him.

He took the towel, drying D as they moved, licking and sucking at the drops of water the cloth missed. D's rumbling purrs turned into growls, the sounds low and deep, he recognized them as arousal, need, care.

They settled in D's nest, D curled around him, warm, rumbling. Safe.

# Chapter 5

Fall was quickly turning into winter, November marking the time when the longer nights found him hunting more often, the urges to feed and fuck strong under the moon's gaze.

Drakon would make love to Matthew and then take to the woods as soon as the boy was asleep, coming back before dawn to shower and then slide into bed with his Pet.

He lazed during the days, dozing and sleeping curled around Matthew, who would read or listen to music.

He'd found that as long as he was touching the boy, Matthew seemed content.

This night he'd had to venture further afield for his meal, the cold driving people out of the forests and into their homes. Lucky for him, the cars they drove were not very well built machines, and there was always a victim to be found somewhere along the road. Still, he'd had to go further, and dawn was already upon him when he got back, one hunger sated, another awoken.

Matthew wasn't in bed, the sheets cool and neatly drawn up. The scent of his Pet still lingered, warm and necessary, filling his nose.

He followed the trail to the swimming pool,

only realizing as he caught sight of Matthew doing laps that he had failed to wash. Oh well, he wasn't too bloody, having been caught in the rain.

Matthew swam fiercely, one lap after another, lean body pale as it moved, the only real color that hair and the blue-black of his mark on that hip.

Drakon stripped away his tattered clothes, leaving them in a corner for Wetthers to deal with, and then slipped into the water. He wondered what demons drove Matthew in his swimming, suspected he was one of them.

Matt took a corner and flipped onto his back, panting as his arms worked, cheeks flushed. Drakon began to move through the water, swimming lazily alongside his Pet. The steady strokes faltered a bit when Matt saw him, then evened out, moving with him, with his rhythm.

He moved closer, arm sliding against Matthew each time he took a stroke. Despite the cold water he was hard, his hunger still strong.

He heard Matt's quiet chuckle, then Matt's thigh started brushing against his. He growled happily, increasing their contact as they turned and completed the lap in the other direction. By the time the lap was finished, they were touching almost continuously, working together.

He maneuvered himself until he was beneath Matt, supporting most of his Pet's weight. He took a kiss.

"Hey D." Matt gave him a quiet smile. "You're a good swimmer."

"It is an exercise I enjoy." He pulled them through the water, licking at Matthew's lips.

"Me, too. I was on the swim team in school." Matthew's hands moved over his sides, his chest.

"Mmm... all those lithe young bodies..."

"Pervert."

He laughed, surprised, delighted. "Me?"

Matthew chuckled, nodded. "Oh, yeah. You. No question. Pure pervert."

"I imagine you're right." He grinned and bit at Matthew's sweet lips.

He received one soft kiss, then another. "My mom called yesterday, D. She wants us to come home for Thanksgiving or Christmas."

He growled. "What did you tell her?"

"The truth." Matt shrugged. "That I'd have to discuss it with you first, see what your plans were."

He growled again, floating as he stroked Matthew's back. "My only plans are to ravish you again and again." He nipped at Matthew's lips, not quite hard enough to draw blood. "I'm not sure she would approve."

"No. I'm pretty sure she'd get pissed." Matt shook his head. "I guess that means you won't come, huh? Well, I'll go home for Thanksgiving, then. I don't want to leave you for Christmas. That wouldn't be fun at all."

"I'm not comfortable with you leaving me, Pet." Perhaps it wasn't fair, but he couldn't risk it, couldn't have Matthew away from him like that.

"Why? I won't tell about the... the..." Matthew tensed, frowned. "I wouldn't."

"It isn't that, Pet. I would pine." He slid his hands along Matthew's back, trying to soothe.

"Pine?" Matt lifted his head a little. "I've only been here... five months. Wow. Five months. Time goes by so strangely in here, you know. The days blend together."

"They do. I have never been happier than I am

now with you, Pet."

He got a grin, thin cheeks pinking. "Really? I... Thank you."

"Really, Matthew." He started to swim toward the edge, patience disappearing quickly. He wanted his Pet now.

"Time to get out?" Matt stretched and climbed up the ladder, water sliding from his Pet's nude body. The yellow-green eyes caught his ruined clothes and steadfastly looked away, the slightest shiver visible.

He growled lightly, climbing out and bending to lick the water from Matthew's skin. He would have to try to remember to leave his clothes in the kitchen. Matt stumbled forward, shuddering again, this time with a moan that was filled with arousal.

He wrapped his arms around Matthew's waist, bringing their bodies together, growling as his Pet's heat met his own.

"Hot... D." Bright eyes met his. "Need you. 's like an ache. Deep."

"I know, Pet. I feel the same ache. If we were to be parted..." He shook his head. Taking Matthew's mouth, he kissed his Pet until they were both quite breathless.

Matt crawled up his body, hands tangling in his hair, teeth just scraping his jaw. "Take me. No more waiting. I can feel you, feel your hunger."

He shuddered, cock throbbing with need. Grabbing Matthew's ass, he spread the lovely cheeks, thumbs sliding into perfect tight heat. A moan sounded, Matt clenching around him, lips begging for more.

He bit at the swollen lips, licking and kissing, thumbs sliding from his Pet's body.

"Mine," he growled, pushing inside Matthew's heat.

Matthew arched, grinding down towards him, his Pet's passion meeting him full-force. It made him roar, made him push hard and deep, taking what was his with a passion only Matthew had ever drawn from him.

Matthew pressed closer, pressed harder, needy cries filling the air. The vision was burned into his eyes, his Pet undulating, driving that thin body onto his cock over and over, pale and perfect, blood smeared on the kiss-swollen lips.

He roared, shaft throbbing within its silky lined prison as he came, pushing his seed deep within Matthew's body.

"D!" He heard Matt's cry from far away, felt the soft body clench around him.

He collected the semen on their stomachs, spread it on Matthew's lips, watched it mingle with the drops of blood and then licked them off together. His Pet's semen and blood -- the essential fluids of life. They were his. Matthew was his.

Matthew cuddled in his arms, eyes closed and shadowed, lips clinging to his.

He slid from the sweet body and carried Matthew up to his bed.

\*\*\*

Matt was sitting at the dinner table working a crossword and thinking.

He was going to have to go home and visit. Mom was insisting, and Dad was still nine tenths pissed off about school, and his brother... well, Scott would have enough to say about the whole gay thing without worrying about school.

Of course, Matt could just tell them that he was in love with someone who was -- at best -- a shape-shifting lizard with a huge appetite.

He hadn't figured out how much worse having a boyfriend who was a filthy-rich, cannibalistic serial killer who thought he was a dragon would go over.

Oh God, he was so utterly fucked.

Wetthers wandered in with a cup of tea and a plate of cookies, and Matthew grinned, worry and stress set aside for a moment. "You're going to make me fat."

"Nonsense, sir. You swim far too often for that to become a worry." Wetthers gave him a small smile. "I quite enjoy having someone who enjoys my baking in residence."

"Baking in..." Matthew frowned and took a sip of tea, wheels spinning like mad in his head. "Hey, Wetthers? Does D ever have company? I mean, here?"

"Very rarely, though it has happened in the time that I have been with him."

"Hmm. Would you be able to cook Thanksgiving dinner for my family if they came? I could help." He wrinkled his nose. "Well, except for the dead bird part. Ew."

"Of course I could, sir." Wetthers pulled out a chair. "May I?"

"Yes. Sure. Please." Matt put the puzzle aside and offered Wetthers a smile. "Want a cookie?"

"Perhaps just one."

Wetthers sat and nibbled at the cookie. "I have purchased a number of vegetarian cookbooks in the past months, and I am quite certain one of them had a vegetarian Thanksgiving meal."

"Yeah? 'cause one way or the other I'm going to be here Thanksgiving, and I'm hoping to invite my folks." Matt sipped at his tea, the heat filling his belly, relaxing and good. "I'd be willing to help."

Wetthers chuckled. "If your family is here, Master Matthew, I would imagine you would do best keeping the peace between them and Master Drakon. I do not mind cooking unless you mean to invite a horde, and then I believe you will find the Master protesting before I do."

"Only three people and my folks are cool. Mostly. Well, my brother's a bit of a pain in the ass, but still okay." He offered Wetthers a grin. "Can we have cherry pie?"

"You may have anything you like, Master Matthew -- you've only to ask." Wetthers small smile returned his grin. "Contrary to the Master's oft-held belief, I am not a mind reader."

"No? I don't believe it." He laughed and nodded. "I'll talk to D and see what he says, and then we can plan supper. Will you eat with us? I hate thinking about you holidaying alone..."

Wetthers looked surprised for a moment before the usual calm mask returned to his face. "If I eat with you, who will serve?"

"We'll do it family style. All the dishes on the table and we'll pass them around." Matthew smiled over. "It's Thanksgiving, Wetthers. You have to celebrate with us."

"If the Master allows, sir, I would be pleased to join you at your table."

Wetthers stood then, wiping a crumb from the corner of his mouth. "In the meantime I have a soufflé needing my attention."

"Ooh! A soufflé? Wetthers? You rock, man."

There was a twinkle in the old man's eyes. "I do try, sir."

Matthew's laughter lasted all the way up the stairs to grab a shower before D woke up.

***

Drakon growled and paced through the dining room, glaring at Wetthers as the man set the table for Thanksgiving dinner.

He couldn't even remember agreeing to this -- his Pet had bamboozled him somehow, and he was pretty sure Wetthers had been in on it.

And now he was dressed up in his best leggings, blouse and cravat -- the leather boots the only part of his ensemble he was happy to be wearing -- with Matthew's parents and brother barreling down upon them.

He was going to have to make nice and smile at people who were no doubt furious at him for taking their dear boy away from his studies. Not to mention the pretending to enjoy whatever foul concoction Wetthers had come up with for these people to eat. He sniffed. He had a hunch it was not meat. A dead, cooked animal would have been barbaric enough, but to force him to eat smashed beans masquerading as dead, cooked animal...

He was almost positive he had most emphatically not agreed to this.

The damned cravat was going to suffocate him.

With another growl he tore it from his neck.

"Would you like me to retie that for you, Sir?" Wetthers sounded calm and cool, damn him.

"No," he snarled, throwing the offending silk into the fire. And missing.

Matthew came in wearing a turtleneck and slacks that hid every mark, curls tamed and forced into straight lines. Drakon hated it.

"If you don't want to wear the tie, D, don't. You look wonderful." Matthew moved over to him and kissed him. "Thank you."

"It feels like a noose."

He pulled Matthew in, body responding to his Pet despite his sulking. "Did you have to do that to your hair?"

Matthew kissed the hollow of his throat. "Probably not. Dad will mention that I need a hair-cut almost immediately, but it might keep Mom quiet for a little while."

He growled a little. "Are you *sure* I can't eat them?"

He might not remember agreeing to this little get together, but he did distinctly remember promising to be on his best behavior and that *that* somehow included 'no eating your boyfriend's family'.

"Not Mom and Dad, D. Scott? He's still up for grabs." Matt grinned up at him. "They'll be here one night, D. Then they're all going to San Jose to meet Scott's girlfriend's folks. It'll be okay. I promise."

He made an unhappy noise, pulling the edge of Matthew's collar down, growls turning happy at the sight of one of his bite marks. He bent and began to lick at it. Maybe he could do something about the boy's hair at least.

Matt stretched, moaning at the touch of his tongue. "D... You're going to make me hard..."

"That's the idea, Pet." He grabbed Matthew's buttocks and pulled him close, let his Pet feel his own need.

"Oh..." Matt's gasp was sweet, the undulations of that thin body sweeter.

This was better.

He bit at the mark, growling softly. "I want you, Pet."

"But..." Matthew looked up at the clock. "I want you, too. Do we have time?"

He picked his Pet up and headed for bed. "Wetthers can answer the door."

"Oh." Matthew chuckled, licked the hollow beneath his ear. "Hungry D."

"For you, Pet? Always." He growled, moving more quickly, getting them into his bedroom. Hunger true and fierce.

Once he had Matthew in his bed, he pulled at the offensive clothes.

"Don't tear them. I have to wear them tonight." Matthew giggled, pushing away the ugly slacks and tugging the turtleneck off, curls springing free.

"Oh, there's my Pet." He pounced, pushing the clothes off the bed and taking Matthew's mouth. His fingers running through Matthew's hair, letting the curls run every which way.

Matthew's laughter tickled his lips, the essence of pure joy sweet and delectable as it was fed to him.

He tore his own clothing off, tossing it over the side of the bed and pressed against Matthew's skin.

"Oh... Yeah, 's good, D." Matthew took a kiss, eyes dancing for him.

He growled happily, nibbling at Matthew's collarbone.

"Mmm..." Matt's lips traced along his forehead, his eyebrows, soft, chaste kisses.

He found the oil with his hand, dipping two fingers into the small pot that had magically appeared one day, and slid them into Matthew's hot body.

"Oh... D. Yes." Matt pulled his legs up, exposing himself, offering himself.

He slid down his Pet's body, tongue sliding along the crease where thigh met groin, biting at the sweet, smooth skin of Matthew's inner thigh as his fingers prepared his Pet for his possession. Matt rode his fingers easily, eagerly; his Pet's passion growing as each day passed. He bit and nibbled, grazed the thin skin until he could pick up a few drops of blood, taking the taste of his Pet into him before moving to lie between Matthew's legs.

"Ready, Pet?" he whispered into Matthew's ear.

"Always. Need you."

Growling, he took Matthew hard, sinking into the tight passage that seemed to draw him in eagerly, pulling him deep. Matthew met each thrust with one of his own, low cries filling the air, hands grasping at him.

Everything he threw at Matthew, his Pet took, meeting his passion eagerly again and again. He growled, the sounds getting louder as he got closer.

Matthew started working the sweet, hard cock, pulling hard, ass clenching in time with their thrusts. Drakon bit at the sweet neck, finding a patch of unmarked skin to sink his teeth into.

"D!" The scent of his Pet's seed filled the air, sharp in his nose.

The heat around his cock rippled and squeezed him and he roared, coming hard.

Matthew panted, snuggling against him. "Mmm... 's *so* good."

He growled in agreement, holding Matthew close. "I don't suppose we can spend the evening doing this instead of having Thanksgiving dinner?"

"Oh, I wish, but this will get Mom off my ass, and then we'll have Christmas. Just us." Matthew kissed him, licking at his lips. "And my birthday, too."

"Good. I'm holding you to that, Pet."

"I promise."

He nibbled at Matthew's collarbone, fingers sliding over the lightly muscled stomach, concentrating on his Pet rather than the ordeal to come.

Matthew was melted, relaxed, almost purring when the doorbell sounded and those beautiful eyes popped open in sheer panic. "Oh, shit!"

Perfect. There was no way Matthew was going to be able to put his hair to rights.

"Relax, Pet -- Wetthers will get the door, and by the time he's served them drinks, you'll be presentable again." He wondered how long he could stall his own getting dressed before stretching the bounds of politeness too far.

By the time they got downstairs, Matt bullying him into his clothes and pulling on the turtleneck, three strangers' scents were in his house.

He growled. "She's wearing *perfume*."

"She's a *mom*, D. They do that. Be good. Don't *growl* at them." He glared over at Matt, who grinned and blushed. "It'll make me hard and that's embarrassing, okay?"

"Oh." He growled just a little, watching the blush increase in his Pet's cheeks, a warning look in those lovely eyes.

"I'll be good," he promised. "Just don't make me eat."

"Fair deal. You ready to be smooth and debonair, D?"

"I am ready to charm the chastity belt off a virgin."

Matthew's happy laughter preceded them into the drawing room.

\*\*\*

Immediately Drakon could see where his Pet got his hair. Matthew's mother was greying, but her curls still hinted at brightness. The men that sat together were carbon copies -- son following father's dark hair and eyes, and stern features.

"Matthew!" The mother stood, running towards his Pet, hands outstretched. It was all he could do not to snarl at her.

"Mom. Hey! You found us!" The woman got a long hug and a quick kiss, then those eyes flashed back at him. "Mom, this is D. D, this is Helen."

He forced his face into a smile, hoped it wasn't too toothy, though it could have been as he was still fighting the snarl. She'd gotten her perfume all over him. Claiming his Pet as her own.

He put his arm around Matthew's shoulders, staking his own claim, taking her hand in his free one and bringing it to his mouth for a bite.

No, a kiss.

He gave her hand a kiss.

"What a pleasure to meet you, Madame."

"Hello, Mr. ...D?" Her concern and worry was threaded through her voice. "I've been dying to meet the man who seduced my youngest from school."

Matthew frowned. "Stop it, Mom. Be nice. His name is Drakon. Drakon, this is my father, Les, and brother, Scott."

He gave them both a short bow. "Les. Scott."

Was this never going to be over? He began to growl, stopping the sound in his throat.

The father gave him a nod, then looked at Matt. "Son. Good to see you."

The brother stood, came over to pop Matthew on the shoulder, grinning wide. "Damn, Blinky! You skip out on school and end up in a damned mansion. Not bad."

Matthew rubbed his arm and shook his head. "Hey, Scott. How's Lisa?"

"Heather."

"Heather?"

The brother nodded. "Lisa didn't put out."

Matthew and Helen spoke at the same time. "Scott!"

He was about to reply "but I bet he didn't eat her", but thought better of it at the last minute, changing the words to, "Has everyone got something to drink?"

The inane chatter went on and on, Helen asking questions, Les rumbling about his Pet's hair, and if that Scott person went to hit Matthew again, D was going to rip his arm off and eat it.

Finally, blessedly, Wetthers called them to dinner.

Matt's whisper sounded as they stood. "Remember, D. You don't have to eat a thing."

"A shame," he whispered back. "I doubt anyone would notice if your brother went missing."

Matthew's giggles were sweet, true. Almost enough to make it worth sitting through the family dinner.

Almost.

***

Matthew almost crawled up the stairs, emotionally and spiritually exhausted.

The family had cornered him when Drakon excused himself -- Mom crying and Scott bitching and Dad worrying. Finally he'd just stopped defending and let them fuss, escaping to the stairs and his D as soon as he could.

He opened the bedroom door, blinking against the darkness. "D? You here?"

The low growl came out of the darkness, enveloping him in his D's presence.

"Oh. You are." He shut the door behind him. "They're all in bed."

"Thank the Stars!" Arms slid around his waist from behind him, D's mouth sliding over the skin of his neck.

"Yes. God, that was awful." He leaned into his lover's arms, relaxing. "How're you?"

D growled again, the sound annoyed.

Matt reached back to touch, to stroke. "I'm sorry. Want to take a shower? I'm sticky."

"Are you sure? I intend on making you sticky again."

"That's a good sticky, though." Matt started moving them toward the bathroom, tugging gently.

"Are you trying to seduce me, Matthew?"

He tilted his head, thinking about it. "No. Seducing is slow and purring and sweet. I'm being pushy." He kept moving them towards the shower.

D laughed, the sound rich, arousing.

His lover let himself be led, and then as Matt climbed into the tub, he was slammed up against the tile, mouth taken hard.

Oh.

He pushed back, lips parting, arms sliding over so-hot skin. D was naked, body warm, hard and solid against him, fingers tearing at his clothes.

"Murder on my wardrobe, D." He ran his fingers through D's hair, chuckling.

"I'll replace it," growled D, teeth and tongue running along his jaw and down his neck.

"Oh. Okay..." He lifted his chin, moaning. His fingers slid down D's belly, cupping the heavy balls.

D growled, and his pants went the same way as his top, D's hands hard on him.

"Hungry..." He got himself completely naked, fingers reaching for the sensitive spots on his dragon.

The growls increased, D's teeth biting deeper. The longer he stayed with D, the more he was marked, D's claws and teeth claiming him over and over.

D was fierce tonight, hunger and need marking him. "Mine, Matthew. They can't have you."

"They just love me, D. I'm their son." He tried to soothe his lover, kissing and petting.

"But you are *my* Pet." D turned him, pushed him against the wall, two fingers sliding into him.

"Yes. And you're my D." He arched back, pushing onto D's fingers.

"Yes," growled D, fingers sliding away, thick cock pushing in.

"Oh..." He threw his head back, crying out, only remembering at the last moment that they had company.

The thrusts were hard, the claiming fast, true. His cries were echoing against the tile, fingers

scrabbling as his body shuddered. D's hands were
hard on his hips, mouth at his shoulder, sucking
and biting. The roar began as vibrations against his
skin, slowly growing strength, volume.

Oh, God. They were going to hear. Oh. Oh,
fuck. Matthew shuddered, throwing himself into
the sensation with all he was.

One of D's hands wrapped around his cock, D
demanding his orgasm. He jerked hard, his cry
mingling with D's roar, seed splashing over his
lover's hand. D's heat burned inside him, filling
him, marking him as surely as the teeth on the skin
of his shoulder.

He gasped, shivering. "Oh, God. D. That was...
Oh. You think they heard?"

D purred, nuzzling his neck, hands warm and
solid on him. "I don't care."

"Mmm... Keep making that noise and neither
will I."

D did, the vibrations of the sound moving from
D's chest to Matt's back.

Matthew moaned, snuggling against the feeling,
the purr soothing him deep, washing away... everything. Everything but D.

D leaned them over and turned on the water,
hands spreading him with soap and then rinsing it
away again. Then he was toweled off, and after
that carried to D's bed, laid out in the middle of it.

He reached for his D, his lover. "My Drakon."

D purred for him again, curled around him.
"Yes, Matthew. Yours."

Matt found his spot, hands sliding over the
warm, smooth skin, petting and stroking, loving D
with his fingers.

D's purrs flowed over him, holding him as

surely as the arms around him. Keeping him safe. Keeping him home.

Where he belonged.

\*\*\*

Drakon got out of bed around two in the afternoon. He took a shower -- a long shower -- and spent quite some time grooming, possibly quite a bit more time than usual. With any luck, Matthew's family would have already gone.

He headed down the stairs, eager to see his Pet.

He found Matt curled up in his favorite chair, napping. His Pet was dressed in jeans and a heavy sweater, curls slowly escaping from the elastic that had trapped them. Drakon leaned over, pulling at the elastic and letting the rest of Matt's hair spring free. That was better.

Matthew murmured, curling up tighter, a soft smile on that face.

He purred, crouching next to his Pet and gently stroking the soft cheek, wanting the closeness. Needing it.

"Mmm... my D." Matthew nestled into his touch, arms opening for him immediately.

He growled happily, picking Matthew up and settling with the boy in his lap.

Matt snuggled close, a soft pseudo-purr sounding. Drakon could still smell the hints of the outsiders on Matt, on the clothes. Places where his Pet had been hugged, held, the hint of mother's tears.

"They're gone?" he asked, fingers sliding beneath the sweater to pull it off.

"Hm-mmm. About noon." Matthew lifted his arms, letting him tug the sweater away. "We all

A Private Hunger

survived. Go us. I think Mom almost likes you, even."

"Really?" He nuzzled the sweet neck, nosing pushing against the marks he'd left. "What did I do wrong?" he teased.

Matthew chuckled, shifting a little. "I don't think she heard us last night. She said you sounded like a gentleman."

He snorted. "Definitely didn't hear us last night, then -- in my experience gentlemen don't roar. They squeak." He drew back and winked at his Pet before taking the sweet mouth with his own.

Matthew's laughter tickled his lips, tasted addictive. Almost as addictive as those fingers sliding deep into his hair and petting his scalp. He purred, need coming upon him swift and hard.

"Want you," he growled into Matthew's mouth.

"You're always so hungry, D." Matthew pressed against him, eyes warm and teasing, hands touching his nape, the hollow beneath his ear.

"For you, sweet Matthew? Always." He growled lightly, pulling Matthew against him so that his Pet could feel his need.

"Mmm... So hot, D." Matthew licked his lips, playful and quick, yellow-green eyes dancing as those thin hips rubbed.

The tenor of his growls changed as he chased Matt's tongue down.

Matt wiggled, slid down off his lap, offering him a chase, offering to play. He grinned, baring his teeth, utterly delighted.

"I'll count to ten."

"Twenty."

He laughed. "Fifteen. Starting now. One..."

Matthew gave him a wild grin and took off,

happy laughter trailing behind.

He finished counting to fifteen and got up, heading out the door into the main hall. He put his head back and breathed in, searching out his Pet's scent. He was delighted Matthew wanted to play. And incredibly turned on.

The game was easier than it might otherwise have been -- the house was full of Matthew's scent, but at the moment, it was also lousy with the scent of the interlopers, so it was easy to find the fresh scents left by his Pet and follow them.

He followed Matthew towards the pool -- they *always* thought the water would confuse him -- and then back up the back stairs towards the bedrooms. He was anticipating pouncing his Pet and perhaps Matthew too was anticipating being pounced, going for a bed as a nice soft landing spot.

Matt led him to his own room, his nest, his sanctuary. His Pet was trying to slide into the closet when he opened the door.

The sight of his Pet inflamed him and with a low growl, he was across the room. Matt scrambled, landing on the mattress as D caught one ankle, holding on tight. He growled, pulling off Matthew's sneakers and gnawing playfully on his Pet's feet.

Matthew squealed, laughing and twisting in his hands. "Tickles! Tickles! Love! D!"

Grinning, he nipped at the tendons along Matthew's ankle, putting his teeth behind the bite.

That got him a squeak, a low cry. "Toothy bastard."

He growled in response and slid his teeth up as far as he could push Matthew's jeans. Which wasn't far enough. With another growl he grabbed the

waist band and pulled, splitting the material along
the seams.

"Damn!" Matthew jumped and glared down.
"Those were brand new, D. New! You've got to
stop wrecking my clothes!"

"Buy more," he ordered, taking bites that didn't
quite break the skin from Matthew's thighs and
hips, breathing deeply the scent of his Pet's need.

"If you eat me, I'm going to be cross." Still,
there was no fear in his Pet. None. Matt trusted
him, believed in him.

He laughed. "If I eat you, I can't make love to
you." He ran his nose along the length of Matthew's shaft, enjoying the heat, the smell. He licked
the sweetly bitter drops from the tip.

"Mmm... your tongue's so hot, like getting
licked by fire." Matthew reached for him, curling
around him.

He growled, lapping at Matthew's prick until he
couldn't stand it anymore and swallowed the boy's
shaft whole.

"D!" Matt arched, shaking hard, cock pushing
into his throat, hands hard on his shoulders.

His sounds slid around Matthew's shaft as he
sucked hard, hand coming up to cup his Pet's warm
balls, fingers playing with them not quite gently.
His Pet made harsh, needy sounds, those pale legs
moving almost like they were swimming in his
bed. He slid his hand back, releasing Matthew's
balls in favor of pushing a finger into his Pet's tight
hole. He would have the proof of his Pet's passion
inside him.

"Oh. Oh, please. D. More. More." Matt started
rocking, meeting his passion head-on.

He growled and sucked harder, pushing a second finger in alongside the first. It took nothing before his Pet spent for him, seed splashing on his tongue. He swallowed it down and then licked the spent prick thoroughly, making sure he got it all.

Matthew gave soft little cries, sated and dazed.

He worked his way up Matthew's body, taking sucking kisses as he went, leaving behind light marks on pale skin. Matthew was blinking at him, lips parted, still panting. He took his Pet's mouth, bringing that sweet breath into himself, devouring and sharing Matthew's own taste with the boy. Matthew kissed him back, one cool hand wrapping around his shaft, stroking him, petting him.

He purred into Matthew's mouth, moving into the sweet hand. "Harder," he growled.

Matthew's hand tightened, kiss gaining an edge. He growled again, hips pushing hard into Matthew's hold. His hands slid along his Pet's back, settling on the birthmark.

"Burns. Fuck, D. It burns when you touch it..." Matthew's eyes were blazing. "Can you feel it, too?"

He nodded, his pleasure increasing at the tingles beneath his fingertips, where they stroked against Matthew's birthmark. The fingers on his shaft worked harder, faster, Matt crying out against his lips.

He roared, pushing hard into Matthew's hand as he came, his own scent mingling with Matthew's.

He panted, shaking his head to clear it. Matthew brought that come-slick hand up and started to lick it clean, tongue pink on the pale skin. He vocalized with more growls, a shudder of pleasure going through him. Those wild eyes watched him, the room filled with moaning as Matt licked his own hand clean of seed.

In that moment, he knew that Matthew was well and truly his.

Putting his head back, he roared.

# Chapter 6

"I'm going to town, Wetthers, before the storms hit. I need more books and to get D his Christmas presents." Matthew pulled on his coat and hat, whistling. Almost his birthday. Almost Christmas. Only three weeks.

"Shall I run you in, Master Matthew?"

"Oh, I can make it. I'll bike down and take a cab back, if the presents are big."

He grinned and grabbed his backpack. Wetthers was busy... being Wetthers, and Matt wanted out in the air before things got too chilly. Besides, Wetthers needed a present, too. Maybe a cook-book. Or a CD.

Nah. Gift certificate.

"Very well. Please remember the Master worries about you when you are not here, and try to be back by dark."

"I will, Wetthers. I promise." He grinned. Wetthers worried so much.

Wetthers gave him a look and then continued through to the kitchen.

Matt headed down the road, whistling. The wind was blowing, the sky grey and gloomy. He headed to town, hitting the bookstore, stopping by the restaurant to visit his friends. Then he found D a pair of bronze clasps for the long hair and headed home, pedaling to beat the growing storm.

As he got close to the estate, he thought he saw something in the woods beside the road. His pedaling stuttered and a cold chill blew up his spine, colder than the wind. Matthew shivered and pushed harder. Home. He wanted to get home.

There was definitely something in the forest. Some huge animal, pacing him. Oh, fuck. Matthew whimpered and kept going. Focusing on heading home, on letting the storm push him faster and farther.

He was nearly home when the... beast broke out of the trees, beating him to the garage. Matthew stood still, breath coming quick and hard, eyes not believing what he was seeing. The beast was tall, wide, skin dark or perhaps covered in scales. There were claws and huge teeth and wild eyes. Torn clothes hung off the beast like rags.

D's clothes.

"D." The bike fell to the ground, the packages tumbling everywhere. Matt could hear his heart beat, his breath, both going faster and faster, slamming inside him.

It occurred to him that maybe he'd just stroke out and die.

Maybe that would be okay.

The beast seemed to almost shimmer and tremble, and it just kind of changed right in front of his eyes. D stood in front of him, mostly naked, hair wild, eyes still glowing, but otherwise, just D.

"Matthew."

Okay.

Okay.

Matthew bent down and picked up his packages, blinking hard against the bright sparkles in his vision. Okay. He was okay.

D's hand slid up along his spine. "Matthew."

He closed his eyes for a second, then nodded. "Y...yeah, D?"

"Let me help you."

D's picked up some of his packages, hand still on his arm, warm, familiar.

"Don't." Matthew cleared his throat, shook his head. "Don't look at them. They're presents."

There was a big crack running all the way down his brain. Huge. If he stopped to think now, he would break in two.

"All right." D righted his bike and helped him put the bags into the basket. "Come home, Matthew. You're cold. I'll warm you."

He was cold. Freezing. His hands were shaking so violently he couldn't hold the bike straight, couldn't steer. "There's a storm coming."

"Yes, Pet." D took the bike from him and steered it into the garage, one arm around his shoulders, bringing him along.

He followed without a word, stumbling over the uneven ground, teeth chattering. Wetthers took the packages from them as they made it into the kitchen, saying something about placing them in his room.

"We're taking a shower," D told Wetthers. "Perhaps you could have some food and a good stiff drink waiting for Matthew when we're done. I don't want him taking sick."

"Very good, Sir."

He looked at Wetthers, eyes wide and so dry they clicked when he blinked. "There's a storm c...c...c... A s...storm."

Wetthers nodded and patted his cheek. "I see. Perhaps you'd like that stiff drink before your shower?"

D growled, tugging at his arm. "No. Shower first. I need."

He fell against D's body, skin shrinking where it touched the torn fabric of D's clothes. The ice began to slam against the windows, starting as a series of plinks and growing louder.

D growled again, hands going beneath his shoulders and knees and picking him up. He was carried up to D's bedroom, his lover not saying anything, just bringing him into the bathroom and starting the shower.

He took off his shoes and socks, then watched his fingers work the buttons on his coat. D shrugged out of the rags and then pushed his fingers away and took over the task of undressing him, working quickly, but not ripping them.

He was picked up again, D taking him into the shower, mouth covering his as the hot water began to fall against his skin.

Hot tears slid from his eyes, burning his cheeks as he let D warm him, let D's mouth and need overwhelm the vision that wouldn't leave his brain. D devoured his mouth, hands sliding over him, making his cock jump, making his birthmark tingle and burn. Matthew moaned, head shaking even as his hands pushed into D's hair and held tight.

"Mine," D murmured into his mouth, shifting him, pushing him against the wall and pressing hot need against him.

He shook his head, moaning, holding on.

D growled, stepped back, those strange eyes burning into him. "No, Matthew?"

"No?" He shook his head, trying to clear it. Things were dizzying. "You scared me. I was scared. I just wanted to come home."

"You are home, Matthew. Home. Mine." D was pressed against him again, cock hard along his belly, mouth solid and sure, pulling up a mark on his collarbone.

"Home. You promise?" He pushed closer, clinging to D's strength. "Safe here with my... my dragon?"

"Yes." D's answer was fierce, full of a wild joy.

"Yes." The tears wouldn't stop, but it didn't matter. D had him, and the storm was here, and he was safe. "Yes, D."

D licked at his cheeks, at his lips, hands sliding over his body, grounding him even as he was made to fly. He met D's kiss, tongue pushing inside, pushing deep, arms sliding around strong shoulders to hold on tight. D's hands slid down to cup his buttocks and pull him close, rubbing them together as low growls filled his mouth. Matt wrapped his legs around D's waist, hiding in the steam and golden hair and red-hot need.

Two soap-slicked fingers slid into him, stretching him.

"D." He bit down on the big vein on D's throat, sucking a mark into the skin.

D roared, fingers pulling away, the thick cock pushing in.

Whimpering, Matt gave himself over to the dragon, to their need. To his Drakon.

D's mouth found his, tongue tangling with his as D's prick pushed in and out of him. His eyes were wide open, staring into blue and brown, falling into the glow. D fucked him hard and deep, pressing into him over and over again. Low growls filled the bathroom.

"Yours." He whispered the word as he came, eyes falling closed.

D roared, heat filling him, arms holding him so close. Matt buried his face in D's shoulder, in the wet hair.

"Mine. Safe. Home." D purred, the hot water sliding over them.

Yes. Yes. Matt held on, let D keep him safe and still in the eye of the storm.

\*\*\*

Drakon turned off the water and wrapped Matthew in a big towel before carrying his Pet to his bed. Wetthers had left a tray on the bedside table with a decanter and two glasses, as well as a small plate of nibbles for Matthew. He settled in the middle of the bed, curled around the still, clinging form.

He hadn't meant to appear before Matthew in his dragon form, but as the dragon, he ran on instinct and Matthew *was* his. Growling softly, he slid his hands along Matthew's skin. So pale, his Pet was still shocky, still trying to find a way to understand what had been seen. They all did this, some coped, some went mad fighting the truth. One or two had died of fright.

Matthew would cope, would come through with flying colors. Gentle and sweet, his Pet was also strong deep inside.

Matthew sighed, the sound peaceful, snuggled closer. "Winter is here. Are we going to have a Christmas tree?"

Sean Michael

"If you want." He hadn't had a solstice celebration in ages.

"I do." Yellow-green eyes looked up at him. "Do you love me?"

What an odd question. "Of course I do, Pet. You are here, aren't you?"

Matthew nodded. "I am. Home, right?"

He nodded. "Yes."

"Were you hunting me? Before? Outside?"

"I was hunting, and then I caught the scent of my own. It made me want. Need. I would not hurt you, Matthew. Not even when the dragon has me in its grasp."

"You can smell me?" Matthew was warming, clinging turning into a snuggling. His strong, brave Pet.

"Your scent is forever locked in my nose, Pet. I can smell you, the dragon... when I'm in that form, I can smell you from a very long distance."

"Do I smell good?" Matt's legs twined with his, a soft, happy sigh sounding.

"Nothing smells better than you, Pet." It was true, too. Matthew smelled like home to him. And like his. And the musk of his Pet's arousal... there was nothing to compare.

"Oh... Oh, good." He got a soft, slow smile. Matthew licked at his lips, tasting him.

He purred. "Do I taste good, Pet?"

"Yeah. Wild and hot, hungry." Those eyes shone up at him. "Mine."

His purr turned to growls. "Yes, Matthew. I am."

Matthew nodded, took another kiss. "Does it hurt?"

"You mean becoming the dragon?" He shook

his head. "Needing to feed hurts, needing to mate can when the need is great. But the beast is who I am."

His hair was stroked, petted gently. "Are you scared you'll get caught? You have to make love to me? Really?"

He purred gently. He'd wondered when his Pet's curiosity would overcome the fear and denial. "I am not scared of getting caught -- Wetthers takes good care of me, cleans up after me. And yes, Pet, whenever I can smell you, the need for you is upon me and I must have you -- I *must*."

"I like your purr." Matthew stroked his cheeks, his forehead, the touch comforting both of them. "You don't make the people hurt, right? I mean, you're fast?" Matt blushed. "I saw your teeth. They looked like they could be fast."

He gave Matthew a toothy smile. "I don't make them hurt, Pet. Clean kills. Screams attract attention."

Matthew blinked up at him for a long second and started chuckling. "You ass!"

He got another kiss, this one more playful, more awake. "You know, D, I bet your cholesterol is deadly high... You ought to think about vegetarianism as a lifestyle choice."

He laughed. "I'm sure I've eaten at least one or two vegetarians, Pet."

The laughter was sweet, filling the room, Matthew pinching his hip playfully. "You're incorrigible."

"I try." He drew Matthew's hand to his mouth and nibbled at his Pet's fingers.

Matthew giggled, shifting against him. "Mmm... hungry D."

"Always hungry for you." He growled and nipped a little harder, letting Matthew feel his teeth.

Matt squeaked and mock-glared. "No eating your boyfriend. It's against the rules -- 'specially this close to Christmas."

"Not even a nibble?" he asked, teasing.

"Nope. Not even a nip." Matthew stretched against him, playing back. So resilient, his Pet's faith and trust in him.

"Spoilsport." He bent and let his teeth scrape along Matthew's collarbone.

"Oh!" He felt Matthew's cock jump against his thigh. "None of that either."

"No? And I suppose you won't let me do this either?" He took one of Matthew's nipples between his teeth and bit down.

"D! Oh!" Matthew gasped, the scent of surprise and arousal strong, heady.

He growled, rolling Matthew onto his back and taking biting kisses from the delicious, pale skin. His Pet wriggled, shifting and turning, trying to avoid his teeth. He licked at the hard little nipples, fingers stroking over Matthew's birthmark.

Matthew moaned, shuddering in his arms, body relaxing, melting into his hands. "'s cheating..."

He raised his head. "Cheating? Pet, I'm a dragon. Cheating is par for the course."

"Well, you're going to have to play fair from now on." The challenging words would have had more impact if Matthew hadn't been shuddering in his arms.

"I don't do well with rules, Matthew." He nibbled at one ear.

"No?" Matthew shivered, pale skin peppered

with his marks. His. "You sure?"

"Quite sure." He growled and licked a line from Matthew's neck down to his cock, lapping at the drops sliding from the tip.

"Oh! Oh, D!" Matt stretched, then curled toward him, body caught.

He growled, the flavor of his Pet filling his mouth, making him instantly hard. He swallowed the tip of Matthew's cock between his lips, sucking hard. His Pet gave a series of sharp, needy cries, fingers tangling in his hair. The flavor was wild, wanton, an addiction, especially as the days grew shorter, the solstice closer.

His fingers dug into Matthew's hips, holding his Pet still as he sucked harder and harder, taking the sweet cock in deeper and deeper.

"D!" Matthew's scream was desperate, liquid heat pouring down his throat. He took it all down, filling himself with Matthew's essence.

Growling, he nuzzled Matthew's balls, pushed Matthew's legs open so that he could lick at the darker musk at his Pet's opening. His own scent was still clinging to Matt's skin, the muscles hot, yielding. He licked at the sweet hole and then pushed his tongue inside, opening Matthew easily.

"D... D... Oh, fuck. So *much*. It's so much, D."

He growled and pushed his tongue in deeper, readying his Pet for his possession. Matthew whimpered, hips jerking away from his mouth, his Pet shuddering.

He rose up, taking the sweet mouth, holding Matthew's hips still. "You are mine."

"D..." Matthew pushed against his hands, twisting.

"Tell me."

Those bright eyes flashed up, challenging, his Pet's strength asserting itself.

"Tell me," he demanded, fingers tightening, keeping Matthew still.

Matthew watched him, eyes serious, body still. Unafraid. "I am yours, Drakon."

He bent, placing a soft kiss on swollen lips. "And I am yours." He surged into Matthew's body, taking and giving with a single, deep thrust.

# Chapter 7

Okay. Holiday with D?

Very much about the fucking.

It was two days until his birthday, and he was tired and sore, exhausted and grouchy. He'd started sleeping in his own bed, just to get a break. It was unhealthy, coming so much. Honestly, what if his balls melted?

Or stopped.

What if a guy only had so much in there and then, poof. Desert city.

That would *so* suck.

And not in the 'watch your fucking teeth, D' way, either.

Matt turned the bathwater off, locked the door and settled in with a good book, a cold Coke, and bubbles. Lots of bubbles. Bubblegum scented ones -- damn Wetthers' weird ass sense of humor anyway. "I thought you'd like the Harry Potter ones, sir" his ass.

Now, Star Wars? That would have been cool. Darth Vader wouldn't have had pansy-assed bubblegum scented bubbles.

Someone tried the handle on the door and then knocked. "Pet? Are you in there?"

"Yep. Having a bath. Be out in a bit, D." Shoo

and let me not have a hard-on for a few minutes.

The door handle rattled. "Let me in, Pet. We can share."

"I'm already in up to my neck."

"So you'll dribble on the floor -- Wetthers will clean it." The door handle rattled again. "Pet. I need you."

"D... You just had me. I'm surprised you can even get it up. Your balls have got to ache. *My* balls ache." He muttered and stretched, trying to reach the lock without actually getting out of the tub.

"You don't understand, Matthew -- the solstice is near."

"So? I mean, the days are short and I'm having a birthday. What? Are you pagan?" He got the door unlocked and then slid back under the bubbles. "It's open."

"The longer the nights, the hungrier I am, Matthew. It has always been so." D was gloriously naked, body hard and magnificent. "Oh, scented bubbles!"

"Yup. Wetthers got them for me." His cock jumped and he ignored it. No hard-ons. None.

D made a noise that sounded rather like a snort. "He likes you more than he likes me."

"I made him mushroom soup when he had a cold."

D wrinkled his nose. "Fifty-seven years and I haven't eaten him -- surely that counts for something."

"Err... No, D. Not really. Not when the man washes your shorts." He grinned. D was so... D.

D raised an eyebrow. "I don't wear shorts. Silly, barbaric custom. Clothes as a whole are."

D stepped into the tub. "Move forward, Pet, let me slide in behind you."

"Bossy old man." Still, he scooted forward, proud that his cock was still mostly soft. See? No interest. None.

D growled softly and settled in behind him, one arm wrapping around his middle and pulling him back against the heat of D's body. D's cock was not mostly soft, not at all, and it poked him firmly in the back, a brand along his spine.

Matt pretended not to notice, relaxing back against D, eyes closing. "You're warm."

D's hands slid down along his body, one teasing across his birthmark, the other playing over his belly.

"Be good, D. I'm *relaxing* -- just relaxing."

D nibbled at his shoulder. "I'm hungry, Pet."

"Want some tabbouleh? There's some in the fridge."

D growled. "You *know* what I meant."

"Don't get grumpy with me." Matt frowned. "If you want to snarl, shoo. I'm trying to be in a good mood."

"I wouldn't be grumpy if you'd make love to me."

"That's blackmail." He chuckled, rested his head on D's shoulder.

"Is not." D nuzzled his cheek. "Blackmail is if I say make love to me or I'll eat you."

"Bitch. I told you, it's bad form to eat your boyfriend before his birthday." He stuck his tongue out, almost perfectly sure D wasn't going to eat him.

D's teeth snapped closed right next to his tongue and D growled. "So when *should* I eat my boyfriend, then?"

Shivers crept up his spine and he pulled away, suddenly chilled. "How about not today."

D growled, pulling him back against the warm body. "Relax, Pet, I have no plans to eat you any time soon."

"Oh, that's good to know." He watched the bubbles popping, fading to a thin covering. He liked the thick layer better. D's lips sucked the water from his skin, sliding across his shoulders and his neck.

Matthew suddenly, desperately wanted to go home. Wanted to be in the quiet little ranch style house that smelled like Anais Anais and always had ice cream bars in the freezer and Head and Shoulders in the bathroom.

D growled lightly, the sound vibrating along his back. "Pet?"

"Yeah, D?" He closed his eyes and pulled the plug, letting the cold water out and turning the hot water on.

"What's wrong?"

"Nothing. I'm just... I don't know. Tired. Sore. Homesick. Feeling the beginnings of cabin fever. I don't know." Matthew shrugged. "I should go out, go for a walk, go visit my friends, call my mom."

He looked back at D with a wry grin, winking. "Get a tattoo. Cut my hair. Learn to skydive. You know, stuff."

"Skydive? That isn't safe, Matthew. If you want to temp fate, hide Wetthers' cleaning supplies."

Matt blinked, then started giggling. "Oh! Oh, D! I do love you. I *do*!"

D purred, looking pleased. "Your laughter makes me happy, Pet."

That made him blush, made the chill inside fade. "Yeah? Good." He turned a little, gave D a soft kiss.

D licked his lips as the kiss ended. "*You* make me happy, Matthew. Never doubt that."

"Oh." He grinned, arms wrapping around D's neck. "Oh, thank you, D. Thank you."

Another purr was his answer, D's arms going around him, tugging him closer. He nuzzled D's throat, legs sliding around D's waist. D's cock was still hard, hot, sliding along his belly, making the purrs grow louder.

"My hungry dragon." Matt held D, hands petting the strong back.

"For you, Pet. Always hungry for you." The water slid in the tub with D's movements.

He licked D's neck, fingers tracing and stroking, loving.

"So good," murmured D, hands on his hips, pulling him closer so there was more friction between his belly and D's cock.

"Yes, D. Good." He fastened his lips around D's skin, pulling up a mark, sucking hard.

"Pet!" D roared, come hot as it splashed against his belly before being washed away by the water.

He grinned, licking the dark spot on his lover's throat. "My D."

"Yes, Pet. Yours." D kissed the top of his head, arms holding him close.

He rested against that strength, eyes falling closed as he floated, the scent of D and bubblegum in the air.

\*\*\*

He came back from feeding and went to check Wetthers' arrangements before going up to shower. The cake was in the shape of a storybook dragon, as was the wrapping paper on the gifts. He growled. Wetthers had a damned strange sense of humor. The presents looked nice, though, piled high next to the comfiest chair by the fire in the drawing room. Perfect.

His shower only took him moments and, clean, he went to wake his Pet. Not because he was hungry, but because he was excited to begin his Pet's first birthday with him.

Or so he told himself.

He crawled into bed with Matthew and began to nibble on the tasty neck. Matt giggled, wriggled and laughing softly in his sleep, curls tousled on the pillow. He growled low, happy. So beautiful, his Pet. Such a delight. He nibbled some more, getting a bit of skin between his teeth. A soft squeak sounded, Matt pulling away and pushing closer in the same motion.

"Happy birthday, Pet," he murmured, nibbling at an earlobe.

"Mmm... thank you." Matt cuddled close, humming softly. "Smell good."

"So do you, Pet. So do you." He continued to nibble and nuzzle, sliding his need along Matthew's thigh.

Matt woke up slowly, blinking and nestling, hands sliding over his body, petting him. He kissed Matt, tongue sliding into his Pet's mouth, taking a taste. "We have to start the celebration of your birth in the proper manner."

"Yeah? Cake? You going to sing to me, D?" Matt licked at his lips, humming.

"There is cake and a birthday breakfast and a birthday lunch and a birthday snack, birthday supper, birthday presents and I might be convinced to sing, but that's not how we begin." He grinned down at his Pet, hand sliding over the thin belly and heading south.

Matt chuckled. "No spankings, though. Right?"

He purred. "Not unless you'd like that. Would you like that, Pet?"

"D!" Matt looked up at him, eyes wide.

"What?" he asked, adopting an innocent tone. "I understand it's quite the kink."

"Kink?" Matthew gave him that 'you've got to be kidding, you are *kidding*, right?' look.

"Yes, Pet. You know, whips, handcuffs, spankings, dildos, plugs, fisting... kink."

Matt gave him a long look. "You know, I'm not sure what's weirder -- the fact that you can rattle those off without blushing, or that I don't know what some of them are."

He laughed. Oh, Matthew utterly delighted him. "One day, when you're bored, we can discuss it. In the meantime, do you want that spanking or not?"

"I... No. You're strong. I'd never walk again. I... No." Matthew shook his head, pushing into his arms, cock stiff.

He chuckled, sliding his hand down along Matthew's spine to cup the sweet ass, letting their shafts rub together. "You're sure, Matthew? I would promise not to break the skin."

"Break the... D!" Another jerk and Matthew's ass rocked into his hands, the cool skin smooth and soft against his palms.

So sweet, so smooth. He slid his hand over one rounded ass cheek and then let his hand fly. He didn't spank hard, just enough to make his hand tingle. "How old are you again?"

"I... Twenty. D! Please..."

He hit Matthew's other ass cheek this time, loving the way his Pet's cock jumped. "That's two."

Matt was gasping, pushing into his arms and away from his hands, lips open and hot against his own.

He hit again, this time both cheeks at once, middle finger crashing into Matthew's crease. "Should I stop, Pet?"

Matt cried out, body pushing toward his hands, thighs parting. "Need you."

He growled, pushing Matt onto his back and grabbing the lube. Teasing was one thing, need was quite another.

His Pet drew his legs up and back, exposing that sweet, tight little hole, offering him everything. He slid a slick finger in, moaning as it sank deep.

"More. D. Please." Matt's balls drew up.

He pushed in another finger, opening Matthew quickly and then slicked up his shaft and pushed in. Matt jerked, pushing up into his arms. Those legs wrapped around him and Matt started moving, fucking the beautiful body on his cock. He growled and added his own power to their coupling, thrusting hard.

They moved faster and faster, Matt crying out on his skin, teeth scraping him as the need flared. He roared, slamming into the sweet, willing body. Heat splashed against him, Matthew jerking and crying out for him. He thrust hard one last time, roaring as he came.

His Pet cuddled into his arms, a soft hum

sounding.

"Happy birthday, Matthew."

He shifted, curling around his Pet. "Mmm... Thank you, D. So good."

He purred, stroking the soft, warm skin. Matt snuggled, lapping slowly at him. "Tell me, Pet. What do you most desire for your birthday?"

"I..." Yellow-green eyes flashed up at his. "I... You. I want you."

He purred and took a long, hard kiss. "You have me, Pet."

"Oh, good. Then I want a non-tearable ward-robe."

"Oh, what would be the fun in that?" He nipped at Matthew's neck and nibbled the sweet ear. "How about an unlimited account at that Gappy store you like?"

Matt giggled. "The Gap? Unlimited? Wicked."

He grinned. "You like it? Good. Wetthers said I should give you a copy of the Drakon Compendium, but I told him you'd rather have something a little more modern than that dusty old book."

"Book?" Matthew sat up. "What book?"

"Just an old volume begun many years ago by a young man who was my companion." He watched Matthew closely. "It has been added to over the years."

"Oh!" Those eyes lit up. "Can I read it? I... I told you I was going to study history in school, right? I was."

He grinned and reached under the bed, pulling out the thick, leather-bound volume. It was a deep red in color, tied closed with a black leather belt.

He handed it over. "It is yours, Matthew. And not the first time it has been handed down on the winter solstice."

"Oooh, cool." He got a quick, hard kiss, before Matthew was diving into the tome, fingers sliding over the pages.

He pouted. "I knew I should have waited until later."

Daylight was streaming through the curtains, though; he supposed he could sleep awhile if Matthew was going to insist on reading the damned thing right this very moment.

"Waited? Hmm?" Matthew snuggled into his arms, into the warmth of his body.

He kissed the top of Matthew's forehead and settled, curled around his Pet.

"Happy birthday," he murmured.

He didn't get an answer before he fell asleep, but then he hadn't been expecting one.

\*\*\*

The book was a fascination.

A terrible, terrifying, unbelievable fascination.

Matthew couldn't stop reading, looking at words that were written centuries ago.

Centuries.

About his D.

He wrapped himself in the words, only coming out to wander into Drakon's room and watch him sleep, compare him to the illustrations in the book. Then he would crawl back into his own room, his own bed and read again.

He'd seen it... Seen what D *was*, seen what D did. It had seemed like a dream, like a weird joke that would one day make sense. Like a fairy story and one day he'd wake up.

Now... he wasn't going to wake up. Not ever. Not really. D had... taken him. Claimed him.

And he'd let it happen.

What would D have done if the muggers hadn't attacked him? Would he be in Miami right now? Free, normal, alone?

He turned the pages, burning eyes roaming over the pages again and again.

It was Wetthers' knock at the door that finally tore him away, the sound firm but not loud.

"Y..." He stopped and swallowed, his voice nonexistent. "Yes?"

Wetthers came in with a tray containing tea. "Your birthday breakfast remains uneaten, Master Matthew. And your presents unopened. Or at least most of them." The old man smiled and nodded at the book.

"I'm not hungry yet. Thank you." His fingers trailed over the pages; they felt like ancient skin. "Have you read it?"

Wetthers straightened and got that snooty look on his face. "No, sir, I have not. The book does not belong to me."

"Don't be angry, Wetthers. I didn't know if D had offered, is all." He tried to smile, tried hard. "I'm not trying to piss anybody off. Honest."

"Of course not, Master Matthew. I am not 'pissed off'." Wetthers gave him a smile, proving the words.

"Yeah? Cool." He looked at the older man, turning another page. "Did... did you know any of the other ones? The ones like me?"

"There has never been one like you, sir." Wetthers pointed to the bed, sitting when he nodded his head. "There was a gentleman already with the Master when I joined him, and another who did not stay about thirty years ago." Wetthers shook his head. "On the whole, Master Drakon has been a solitary man."

"What...The one who didn't stay? Did he just leave? Just go home?" He'd read the whole thing, front to back, and each story ended without answering that question.

Still, each story? They stayed with D every day until the story ended.

Every single day.

"I cannot say where he went, sir. One day he was just... gone."

"Oh." He took a deep breath or two and rubbed his goose pimpled arms. "Why did you start working for him? Aren't you lonely?"

"I am a loner by nature, Master Matthew, and rather well-suited to the task of caring for the Master. As to how -- my predecessor discovered me. He must have seen something promising in me."

"Promising? The most perfect butler-type dude on earth? Nah..." He tried to laugh, but it wouldn't work. Not at all. "I...I'm scared. I'm in way over my head, Wetthers, and I don't know what to do."

"Do you love him, sir?"

"Yeah. Yeah. I shouldn't, but I do."

"Then you should trust in that, sir. Go with it. He will care for you for all of your days. I have never wanted, and I am just his man, not his lover."

He nodded. "I guess... I guess sometimes you just have to do that. Go with it." Matt took a deep breath and closed the book, taking the tea and drinking. "So... what's for breakfast? I want to wait for D on the presents, but... Wanna eat with me? I promise to use the right fork and everything."

"The Master asked me to wake him when you were ready to eat. He wishes to spend the entire day with you, be at your disposal as it is your special day." Wetthers stood and gathered the tray. "I've made your favorites."

"Yeah? Thanks." He put the book away in the bedside table, closing it away for now. "I'm going to jump in the shower and I'll be down."

"Then I shall wake the Master." Wetthers went to the door and then turned back, giving him another smile. "I'm glad you're with us, Master Matthew."

"Thank you. I... It's home, yeah? D's home."

"It is indeed, sir. It is indeed."

\*\*\*

He was wearing a fine pair of doeskin leggings and a silk blouse, the top three buttons undone. His hair was brushed and loose along his back. He was barefoot.

He was bored.

Wetthers had woken him almost an hour ago, letting him know his Pet was about ready to finally come down and open his gifts. He grinned. Perhaps Matthew was adjusting to his nocturnal ways.

Still, he was growing impatient. There were presents to unwrap!

At this rate he wouldn't be surprised to discover that Matthew did *not* rip wrappers off his gifts either, but neatly removed them.

"Oh." Matt stood at the door, eyes wide, dressed in a huge green sweater and a pair of jeans, hair all curls. "D. You look... Wow."

He beamed and held out his arms. "Almost as

good as you do, I hope."

He got a grin and then his arms were filled, his Pet's face lifted for a kiss. He took one, keeping it light; there were presents to be opened. "Happy birthday, Matthew."

"Thanks." Matt grinned, belly rumbling. "What's for breakfast?"

"What's your favorite, Pet?" He grinned and rubbed their shafts together. "Aside from me."

Those happy, low, unintentionally sexy giggles started, Matthew pushing closer. "Waffles with blackberry syrup."

He frowned and growled. "That's it, Wetthers is fired -- he made waffles with blueberry syrup!" He winked at his Pet as Wetthers came in with a large tray.

"Waffles and blackberry syrup, sir. Would you like to take it in the chair by the fire?"

Matthew bounced in his arms, hugging tight. "Cool! Yes, please! Oh, wow. Wicked."

"There's presents," he pointed out helpfully as he led Matthew to the big chair.

"Yeah? Can we open and eat at the same time?" Oh, yes. That was definitely bouncing.

He grinned. "Of course -- you can do anything you like, Pet -- it's your birthday."

"Yeah. Almost legal." Matt grinned, looking at the big chair. "How're we going to do this? On your lap?"

"Oh, I do like the way you think, Pet." He slid into the chair and patted his lap.

Matt settled in, leaning down to fix them a plate and then cuddling into his arms, insisting on sharing the sweet, sticky mess. He ate it with good humor, insisting on long kisses in return.

By the time the plate was half eaten, Matt's eyes were wandering to the packages. "Which one first, D?"

"You could start small and work up."

"Cool. Hold me and I'll stretch." His hands wrapped around Matt's hips as his Pet reached out, snagging the smallest present.

He let his hands slide over his Pet's body.

"No distracting, D." Matt took another bite, opening the paper as he chewed.

He pouted. Matt chuckled, leaning up to take a long, sweet kiss. He growled happily, pulling the taste of his Pet into his mouth, sweeter than any syrup. The present was set aside, Matt turning, deepening the kiss.

Oh. Better than a present. Better than a whole pile of presents. He growled happily, pulling Matt close against him. Hands slid into his hair, tugged them together, Matthew's kiss a little desperate, more than a little needy. He could handle that.

He slid his hands beneath Matthew's shirt, stroking over the slim belly, the long spine. Matt moaned into his lips, fingers moving to pet him, stroke him. His own arousal flared and he took control of the kiss, tongue invading Matthew's mouth.

"D..." Matt rocked against him, rubbing, licking, fierce and his.

He pushed Matthew's sweater up over the curls and pulled open the button on his Pet's jeans, hand going in for the hot prick.

"Oh. Yes." Matt pushed up toward his hand, cock sliding along his palm.

He growled, hand wrapping around Matt's heat, mouth taking his Pet's. Sharp cries pushed into his mouth, those bright eyes glittering. His free hand plucked at Matthew's nipples as he continued to tug. He wasn't sure what had gotten into his Pet, what caused this bloom of need, but he would take it, take the desperate motions and the gasping and the want. He fed off them, letting them fill him with his own sweet purrs and Matthew's hungry cries.

"Come for me, Pet," he murmured, thumb stroking across the tip of Matthew's cock, seeking out his Pet's pleasure.

Matthew cried out, arching back, seed spilling over his fingers, hot and rich. He growled happily, bringing his hand up to taste the flavor of his Pet's pleasure.

His arms were filled with melted, sated boy, Matt's tongue sliding over his throat. "So good."

He purred. "Yes."

He kissed the top of Matthew's head, chuckling. "You threw the jewels over for me," he said, nodding toward the small box Matthew had let drop.

"Jewels? D?" Matthew nuzzled closer. "You're good to me."

"Well... one jewel. More or less. Open it."

Matthew opened the box, eyes widening when the ring came into view. It was a gold signet ring with a strong, simple D engraved on top.

He took the ring out of its box and turned it so that Matthew could see the inscription. "To Matthew, my beloved Pet."

"Oh. Oh, wow. D." Matthew slid it on his finger, smiling wide. "Wow."

"You like it, then?"

"It's classy, D. I do." Green eyes twinkled up at him, mischievous and wicked. "Besides, it's *so* much less obvious than a collar."

He threw his head back and laughed. Matthew kissed his throat, settled in to open the rest of the gifts and share the last of the waffles.

There was a sweater from Abercrombie and Fitch, along with a gift card from there and from the Gap.

"You see?" he growled. "Unlimited supply of clothing, so I can tear to get to your skin."

"Impatient beast. It would be cheaper to just wait and let me get naked." Matt's chuckles tasted good.

"But far less fun," he pointed out.

"You're just all claws and teeth."

He raised an eyebrow and pushed his hips forward, nudging his Pet with his cock.

Matthew giggled. "Okay... Maybe there's a *little* more than that..."

"Little?" He growled.

The giggles became full-fledged laughs, Matthew rubbing his cock through the suede. "Mine."

"Yes. And not little."

"I guess that depends on what you're comparing it to, D." Matthew grinned, playful. "I mean, we *know* I'm huge and studly..."

Then his Pet scrambled, running for the door in a mad dash, laughing the whole way.

Oh, he loved it when Matthew played, teasing and taunting and *running*.

It made it so much more fun when he took the boy down.

The chair fell over behind him as he leapt up and gave chase.

# Chapter 8

He'd done everything he was supposed to. He'd applied for admittance for the spring semester. He'd applied for grants. He'd spoken to counselors over the phone, and now it was time to choose classes.

Well, that and remind D.

Matthew took the course catalog and a pad, and curled in front of the fire, humming and making notes and juggling times. Drakon was still sound asleep, still recovering from the pre-solstice hunger weirdness.

English, American history, algebra... Now, anthropology or chemistry...

Wetthers came in with a cup of tea and a plate of chocolate dipped shortbread. "Tea, sir?"

"Oh, cool! Yeah, thanks." He sat up, gave Wetthers a grin. "So what do you think? Anthropology or chemistry?"

One of Wetthers eyebrows went up. "I didn't realize you'd found a correspondence school, Master Matthew."

"A correspondence..." Matt tilted his head and frowned, then blinked. "Oh! No, man. I got into the university. D and I discussed it back in August. That was part of the thing. I didn't go to Miami, I could go to school here."

"Oh. And you haven't discussed it since August?"

"No, not really. I mean, Mom and I talked about it at Thanksgiving and D was there..." He blinked up, frowning. "I got grants to go, and Dad's going to send me enough to buy a little car and books. It shouldn't be a big deal, right? I mean, D sleeps all day..."

Wetthers' face was that neutral, 'I'm not picking sides -- I'm merely pointing out the obvious' look that he sometimes got. "You do remember why you had your family here for Thanksgiving."

"Yeah, 'cause D didn't want to travel and didn't want me gone for the whole week. I got that. I'm not moving into the dorms or anything, Wetthers. I'm just going to a few classes." Surely D wouldn't mind that. Three days a week for a few hours wasn't *anything*. Nothing at all.

"He doesn't like it when you go to town for an hour or two, sir. How do you think he's going to react to you being gone for extended periods of time on a regular basis?" Wetthers gave him a sad smile. "He might surprise us both, but I think it would be best if you prepared yourself for the worst, Master Matthew."

"But..." Matthew blinked hard, gathered up his papers, holding them in suddenly sweaty fingers. "I... I'm going for a walk, Wetthers. I'll be back in before dark."

D had promised he could go to school. D knew he needed to go. D *knew*.

"Very well, sir."

D came down the stairs as he left the drawing room, smiling warmly at him. "Pet! I was just coming to find you."

"Oh? I was just heading out for a walk." He gave D his best smile. "You're up early."

"The bed is empty without you -- your scent only lingers so long before it is not enough and I must have it again from the source." D wrapped warm arms around him, holding him close.

Matt cuddled close -- he wasn't sure how D did it, made him feel warm and safe even when *D* was the reason he was worried.

His papers were pressed between them, and D drew back enough to pluck them away. "What's all this?"

"A catalog from the university." He would *not* be nervous. Not. Not, not, not, not. D had *said* it was okay. "It's time to start picking classes for the winter."

"Ah, you found a correspondence school, wonderful! What courses are you taking, Pet?"

"No, D. It's the university in town. It's a state school, but it's accredited and I got grants to go. They have a good swim team -- one of the coaches was in the Olympics." Matt opened the catalog, flipping pages, pointing out the classes he'd marked. "I'm thinking I'll only do classes three days a week while you're sleeping, and study the other days."

D frowned. "I don't know, Pet. I don't like the idea of you being gone that much."

"You'll not even notice, D. You sleep during the day. If I pick them right, even *with* driving time, I'll only be gone eight to two."

"But I cannot protect you while you aren't here." D shook his head. "I do not want you to do this, Matthew."

Matthew took a deep breath, braced himself. "You said I could, D. Back at the beginning. It was part of the deal, remember?"

He wasn't giving this up. He *wasn't*.

"I would have said anything to make you stay, Pet."

Oh.

"I'm going to school, D. We agreed. I can't just sit here everyday forever." He wasn't used to people just admitting they'd lied without so much as a blink of an eye. It was... weird.

Painful and weird.

"You can buy the books and follow the courses from home," D told him. "Or find someplace that will allow you to use the computer. We'll buy you something top of the line, you can use it for games as well as school work. That will be fun. See, more stuff to do."

"Drakon, the university is twenty minutes from here. Twenty. Forty with bad traffic. Dad's even going to buy me a little used car." He shook his head. "I'm not talking about moving away, love. I'm talking about going to school."

"With all those other people. Don't try to pretend, Pet -- I know there will be many, and they will all want you. They can't have you, though -- you're mine."

"Want me to what? Turn in papers and sign weird petitions? D? Come *on*." He shook his head. "Besides, I love *you*. I'm not looking for anyone else."

"It's not you I'm concerned about, Pet. I trust you." D looked solid, stern. Immovable. "You won't go."

"The paperwork's already done, the grants are

done. You promised me. I'm going." He could be immovable, too. He had a mom. He'd done this before.

"No," D told him. "You are not."

"You're not my fucking father, D. You're my lover. I'm not asking for your permission." Oh, this pissed him off. "I got the money myself. I made the arrangements. I will even set up the classes while you're sleeping, but I'm going to college."

Something almost sad crossed D's face. "I cannot be without you, Pet."

"You're *not*." Matthew took a deep breath, hands raking through his curls. "I'm not *going* anywhere but to town three days a week, D." Oh, he felt sick. Sick and scared and worried and... Well, completely fucking confused would probably work, too.

D sat down hard on the stairs, burying his face in his hands.

"What's wrong?" His spine was tingling, every nerve on edge, aching.

"You do not understand my need, Pet." D looked up at him, eyes blazing. "You do not understand what it will be like for me when you are not here."

"But I go to town now..." Tears filled his eyes and he blinked them back, putting a bit of space between them.

"And I hate it. Every second of it is an eternity." D all but snarled the words at him.

"D... I can't just... No one can spend their whole life in a house. I need to go to school." He took another step back, goose flesh rising over his arms.

"It's better than a dungeon," muttered D.

"What?" Oh, he was going to be sick. He was.

"I'm not your prisoner, am I?"

"That's my point, Matthew. Not all my... companions have been so lucky."

"I need some air, D. I'm going for a walk." He needed to find a quiet place to scream, to figure himself out, to figure out what to do. Fuck.

"Don't be too long, Pet. I have need of you."

"I won't. I'll be in by dark." He walked out, not meeting Wetthers' eyes, not saying another word.

He walked past the labyrinth, past the gardens, down into the forest by the creek. He found a place to sit that wasn't too wet, wasn't too small. It was cold, the snow ankle deep, his light jacket just enough, until the wind started blowing.

Or the tears came.

He wondered idly if he could go, just get on a plane and fly away to... Venezuela or New Guinea or Timbuktu or somewhere. Would it be over? Would D just find another... whatever he was? Would he be free?

Or would D follow him?

Would D go to visit Mom? Or Scott?

Oh, God, he was cold, way deep inside that didn't have *anything* to do with weather.

He had no idea how long it had been, though the sun was low in the sky, when D came trudging through the snow. A blanket was put around his shoulders and D sat next to him. "I was worried about you."

"I'm okay. Just thinking, watching the water."

"It's cold." One warm hand rested on his knee.

"Yeah." He nodded, eyes watching the water beneath the ice.

D sat quietly next to him, hand warming his leg, just there.

The tears started again, slow and steady and silent. His hair hid his face from D, so he didn't stop them, just let them go, let them make him empty and raw inside.

"Pet..." D's arm went around him, pulling him into the solid, warm body. "Sh... Oh, Pet, I hate to see you so unhappy."

"I didn't... didn't even get a choice in this. I... I've worked *hard* to get into school, D. I'm a *man*, not a pet. Not really. I love you. Why does this have to be so hard?" He curled in, shivering now that his body remembered being cold.

"I'm sorry, Pet. Matthew. I would change things if I could."

"I want to go to school. I want to be on a swim team and race. I want to make friends and bring them home to meet my lover."

"Matthew... I'm not the type of lover you bring friends home to meet. You know that. You know why." He was pulled into D's lap.

"I know. I do. I'm not asking for that, D. I'm *not*. I just want to go to school." God, he was whining. Fucking *whining*. "We talked about it right at the beginning. I thought you understood."

"I had Wetthers look into it, Matthew. There are ways for you to take classes without being there. He can arrange it all for you. You don't have to give this up."

He looked up into Drakon's eyes, heart breaking. "I'm never going to get to go home again, am I? Go see Mom or Scott or where I grew up. Go visit anyone."

"I don't travel well, Matthew."

Matthew wanted to scream, wanted to beat D's chest and ask him why? Why of all the people, why pick a scrawny, red-headed dork? It wasn't fair. Then again, whole bunches of things weren't fair, were they?

He could almost hear his mom telling him that. "Life's not fair, son." So he just nodded and stood up and started back to the house, hiding inside the blanket.

D fell in step beside him. They were almost home when his lover stopped. "Is it really so terrible, Pet? Belonging to me?"

"D, I'm a *person*. People don't *belong* to other people. I love you. I want to be with you -- forever -- but I'm not a thing. I'm *me*. You're asking for everyday, not leaving this house, not having a normal life *forever,* and I didn't get to choose." He looked at D. "You weren't ever going to let me go. Not ever. What would you have done? If you hadn't found me? Would you have just let me go?"

"You would have found your way here, somehow, Pe- Matthew. I could feel how you were drawn to me. I knew you were mine and I yours."

"I..." He stopped, then nodded. He'd wanted to come this direction for as long as he remembered. He fought his parents over it -- the first real fight they'd ever had -- and come without a job or a place to live or anything, as soon as school was done.

"Life with me can be wonderful, Matthew, if you are willing to let it be."

"I'm trying, D. I'm trying to work this all out." He sighed, rubbed his temple. God, he was tired.

"I know." D took his head between large hands and kissed his forehead before massaging gently. "I just want you to be happy, Pet. I need you to be happy."

Matthew leaned into those hands, so warm, even after being out here for so long.

Another soft kiss graced his forehead. "Come inside with me, Pet. The sun is gone, the night is cold."

He nodded. "I'm cold."

"Then let me warm you, Matthew."

D picked him up, cradling him against the solid chest and carrying him home.

\*\*\*

It was snowing.

Grey and dim and quiet and cold -- the snow just kept falling, blanketing them in the big house.

Trapping them.

Trapping him.

Christmas Day had come and gone almost without him noticing it. There had been a tree that appeared Christmas Day like magic. Nothing had ever been so perfect -- silver and blue ornaments, white lights, every needle intact, every branch straight. Even the perfect wrapping on the perfect presents matched.

His goofy, Santa paper had looked stupid. Messy. Out-of-place. Wrong. Childish. Ridiculous. So much less than perfect. When Wetthers offered to rewrap them to match, he'd said yes.

Matthew couldn't even remember now when they'd opened the presents, whether the fancy dinner that D didn't eat had been before or after. The laptop was still in the box, sitting on the desk in his room along with everything else.

Mom called late on Christmas night -- he hadn't heard the phone ring, and D was out being D, but

Wetthers brought him the phone and he felt bad
that he hadn't called, that he couldn't call. He talked
to everyone, listened to the crowd of friends and
family laughing, singing carols, playing.

He sat on the tile floor, cradling the phone and
crying, listening to Mom jabber on about silly
things -- the dog and the music and the parties, and
oh, but he must be too busy for family things, D
was so elegant.

"D's a quiet man, Mom. He doesn't get out
much."

"Are you okay, son?"

"Yeah. I... I miss you. I wish... I wish I was
home."

He could see her nodding, see her curls bobbing. "I wish you were home, too, but, hey! You
are home now, aren't you? I mean, you kept telling
us you were where you belonged, right?"

"Yeah, Mom. I... I just..." He sighed. "It's hard."

"Yeah. It is, but that's part of growing up. Stick-
ing it out when it's hard, right?"

He nodded, sniffled. Yeah. Part of growing up.
He'd never thought growing up was going to be so
far outside his control. He'd always thought... It
didn't matter what he'd thought. What mattered was
what *was*.

Every night he went to sleep in his own bed, the
door locked. Every morning he woke up in D's
arms in the master bedroom. Everyday he read a
little, wrote a little, swam until he threw up, then
slept.

Matt could feel Wetthers watching him. Worrying. Waiting for him to crack or scream or break.
He wasn't going to, though. He was going to cope,
to deal, to...

He watched the snow fall, blanketing them. D was out there. Hunting. One day, D would be hunting him. He wasn't ready to feed the beast.

Not yet.

Not today.

"Are you sure you're going to be okay, Matthew? You're worrying me."

He shook his head, brushed his cheeks. "No, I'm okay. I was just looking out the window."

"Oh? Are you planning on going somewhere?"

"No, Mom. It's snowing." He told her he loved her and told her goodbye, leaving the phone for Wetthers to find.

*** 

It was the New Year and Drakon was not sure his Pet wanted to celebrate. Usually humans made a big deal out of this sort of thing, but Matthew was still coming to terms with the sacrifices needed to love him. He decided to have Wetthers bring up a bottle of champagne to chill, only to find that the man had already done so. Really, Wetthers scared him sometimes.

There were also appetizers and little sweets for Matthew.

He thanked Wetthers and went to find his Pet, to see whether they would be celebrating or hiding together in his nest.

Drakon finally found Matthew in the pool, swimming laps with the quiet still determination that the boy had, completely losing himself in the water. Drakon took of his clothes and slid into the water, floating, watching.

Finally, Matt stopped, holding onto the wall,

breathing hard, cheeks flushed dark.

He slid his hand along Matthew's back. "Good Evening, Matthew."

Matthew squeaked and jumped, loosing his grip on the side, sputtering a bit as he came up. "Oh! Oh, you *startled* me, D!" He got a half-grin. "Hey, D. How're you?"

"Good, Matthew, and you?" He pressed up close, purring.

"Okay, I guess. Been working out, took a long nap. Normal stuff."

"It's New Year's Eve." He bent to lick at the water on Matthew's shoulder.

"Yeah? Already? Wow." Matthew looked a little nostalgic for a second and then grinned. "I've got to call Mom tomorrow, it's her birthday."

"Wish her a good one from me," he murmured, hands sliding around to stroke Matthew's belly.

"Mmm..." He felt Matthew shiver, could smell the arousal just beginning to bloom deep inside his Pet. It felt good, pleasure had been a rare scent lately. He continued to lick at Matthew's skin, lips nibbling at his Pet's neck, hand moving slow and easy.

"You got plans for tonight, D?" Matt's eyes closed, the slender body relaxing against him.

"I thought I'd go along with whatever you wanted to do."

"Yeah? Do... Do you dance ever?"

"I can waltz of course, minuet, madrigal..."

Matt tilted his head. "I know about waltzing, not the others. Last year I danced at a club all night, and then this odd little dude kissed me at midnight. I'd like to dance with you." Eyes flashed up at him, quick and almost playful. "I'm not kissing Wetthers, though."

He threw his head back and laughed. Oh, Matthew did delight him so. "I'm sure he'll be relieved to hear it." He teased his fingers along the line of curls at Matthew's groin. "I, however, would love to dance with you. I would also love to kiss you."

Oh, that got him a real smile, those too-pale cheeks warming to a rose, his Pet actually cuddling against him. "Yeah? Cool."

"Wetthers made you munching things. And there's champagne -- one of my best bottles."

"I've never had champagne before." Matt gave him another smile. "I have a new outfit, though. One from Christmas. I could wear it for you."

"That would be wonderful, Matthew. I even promise to try not to tear it."

Matthew turned and grabbed his shoulders, pulling up to whisper into his ear. "It's all lace-up and leather. You'll like it."

Then Matt turned toward the wall to go. "I'll go take a shower."

He growled, reaching out to grab his Pet's waist. "Are you sure we shouldn't take care of a couple of things here first?"

Matthew jerked, gasped, tugging just slightly against his fingers. "What things, D?"

"This for one," he murmured, rubbing his hard shaft against Matthew's ass.

"You don't want to wait? Anticipation and all?" Those pretty, trim thighs parted a little, giving him a glimpse of the pink sac between.

He growled. "I'm not good at waiting."

"What are you good at, D?" The words were part challenge, part tease.

He chuckled, the sound husky, and slid against

Matthew. "What do you think?"

"Hmmm... badminton? Croquet? Tiddlywinks?" By the last, Matthew was fighting the laughter, leaning back towards him, just a little. Flirt.

He goosed the boy.

"*D*!" Matt squeaked, collapsing into husky laughter, just landing fully in his arms, right where his Pet belonged.

He purred, holding Matthew close and nibbling his neck. "Tiddlywinks. I don't even know what tiddlywinks are, though they sound like they'd be crunchy."

"Probably, but they'd upset your stomach." Matt leaned forward, giving him more skin to play with.

He slid his tongue down along the knobbly spine, letting his teeth graze now and then.

"Mmm... my hungry dragon." Matt stretched, sliding along his body. "Don't let me drown, D."

"You're safe, Pet -- I've got you."

An odd look crossed Matt's face, not unpleasant, just... odd. "You do."

"Everything all right, Pet?"

Matthew turned and those eyes met his dead-on. "Can I ask you a question?"

"That sounds ominous, Pet." He kissed Matthew softly. "But you may ask me anything."

"Do you think I'm weak? I mean, I keep thinking and thinking, trying to figure everything out." His Pet shrugged, frowning. "If this was a movie? I'd run away and escape or I'd fight you. I'd sneak around and be brave and clever and go. But, see, the thing is... I'm not. I mean, there's stuff about this that I don't like, that I don't like at all, but... there's you and I shouldn't love you, but I do. And I keep wondering, what's wrong with me? Why am I here? Why don't I run? Why do I keep ending up in your bed when I should be stronger?" Matt looked down, shook his head. "Why am I telling *you* this?"

"You think it's weak to stay with me, Matthew? You think a weak man toys with me, teasing me? Runs knowing he will be caught -- wanting to be?" He gave Matthew a long, hard kiss. "Only the strongest in spirit are as close to being my equal as you are, Matthew."

"You just wait, D. One day I'll kick your butt." He got a grin, those eyes shining, then those fingers slid into his hair, petting his scalp. "Happy New Year, Drakon."

He purred. "You just might, Matthew." He nipped at Matthew's lips again. "Happy New Year."

Legs wrapped around his waist and Matthew pushed close, lips brushing his. "You've got me."

"I do." He wrapped his hands around Matthew's ass, growling softly.

"You going to keep me?" Matthew moaned into his lips, arousal sweet and real.

"I am," he purred.

He took Matthew's mouth, deepening the kiss, pulling his Pet close. Matthew groaned, opening wide, hands tugging them together. The arousal was hot and sweet, the water cool, a sharp contrast to the heat between them. Soft little sounds pushed into his mouth, flavored with need, with love, with delicious desire. He teased Matthew, drawing that sweet tongue into his own mouth. His Pet followed willingly, tongue sliding deep and tasting him.

He sucked on Matt's tongue, growls vibrating in his chest. Matthew's shaft was hard, hot where it rubbed against his belly, wanting him. He shifted, taking it and his own in one hand and stroking them together.

"Oh..." Matt's head fell back, throat working. "More, D. More."

He squeezed tighter, pulled harder, teeth closing over the beating pulse in Matthew's neck.

"Yes..." Matthew arched, shuddering, offering him everything.

Growling, he took what was offered, took Matthew, kept sucking at the salty skin, kept tugging at the hard heat in his hands.

"My D!" Matt's eyes flew open, hips jerking as heat spread between them.

His own heat joined Matthew's before the water washed away the evidence of their pleasure. His suction eased and he began to lick at the dark mark he'd raised on Matthew's skin.

"Mmm... tingles." Matthew relaxed against him, humming and melted.

He nodded, one hand moving to stroke along Matthew's birthmark. A soft noise, almost a purr, but not quite, sounded, tickling his skin. He purred himself, drawing Matthew closer. His Pet. His.

They floated together, Matthew so trusting, so relaxed, that his Pet simply dozed off, cradled between him and the water.

He kept purring, kept floating, holding the most important thing in the world in his arms.

\*\*\*

Matthew had woken up in Drakon's bed, his lover still curled around him and smelling of chlorine. He'd gone to take a long, hot shower and get dressed.

D said they were going to dance.

He pulled on the tight leather pants, using a bit of baby powder to help, and laced the crotch. Then he pulled on the world's softest, warmest knit shirt with matching lacing at the throat. Matt put a little eyeliner on -- not too much, but some, enough to feel sexy. Then he ran his finger through his curls and went downstairs to celebrate the New Year.

D was already down there, wearing a pair of black leather breeches and a white silk blouse. The long blond hair was tied back with one of the clasps he'd given D for Christmas. His lover was standing by the fire, a glass of amber liquid in his hand.

He leaned against the door frame, just watching for a minute or two. "Happy New Year, D."

D turned, smile warm. "Oh, Pet. You look fantastic!"

He grinned, felt his cheeks heat as he turned. "Yeah? You like?"

D growled and the smile grew toothy. "I do."

He was still laughing as he pushed into D's arms, face lifted for a kiss. "You look hot, D. Very classy."

"Oh good, I was hoping I did. I'm going dancing with someone special."

"Yeah? Funny. I am too." Oh, man. D was *too* good at this flirting thing.

"Imagine that." D gave him a soft kiss. "Well, that will be where the difference ends because the someone special I'm meeting is very sexy. He's promised me lace-up pants."

"Wow. Those are sexy. I don't know, though... My date? He growls and has this great belly..." Matt stroked D's stomach, loving the way the muscles rippled through the silk.

D growled, softly, almost purring. "Does he have wonderful red curls?"

"Nope. No silly curls. All gold and heavy. Like silk."

D bent and licked his earlobe. "Mine still sounds better."

"Mine's special, though, and he loves me." Matthew shivered and brushed his lips along D's jaw. This was really fun.

Hot. Sexy. Fun.

"Mine wears my mark," whispered D, hand stroking his birthmark through his clothes.

"Mine wanted me before we even met." His voice was husky, almost like they were doing a spell, him and D, together.

"Mine did, too, he just didn't realize it, yet." D started to move them, not dancing, not really, just sort of... swaying together.

He wrapped his arms around D's waist, humming. "Yeah, D, maybe, but my lover? He invited my mom to Thanksgiving dinner."

D threw his head back and laughed. "Oh, Pet. You win."

Matthew nodded, grinning so hard his face hurt. "You gotta know when to play the mom card, D."

"Brat." D nipped at his nose.

"Am not." Matt stuck out his tongue, licked D's chin.

Oh, yeah. Sexy. Fun.

D chuckled and slid an arm around him, turning him toward the door. "Come on, let's see if Wetthers managed to work yet another miracle."

"A miracle? Are you making Wetthers work on the holiday?"

"He volunteered."

D led him toward the ballroom. "When I came down I mentioned you wanted dancing. You know how he is."

"Yeah, I do." He grinned and nodded. "Wetthers is a good guy. We should send him on vacation."

D gave him a horrified look. "I don't think so."

"No? Maybe a cruise? Chicks, booze, relaxing, no cleaning? Man, Wetthers might want to get laid, D." God, teasing D was fun.

"Get laid? Wetthers? I believe it's against his religion, Pet."

"What? Butlers have a special celibate religion? Did you corrupt a priest, D?" He was *never* going to hold in the giggles at this point.

"I didn't corrupt the man! I've never laid a single finger on him!"

"Poor guy!" He met D's gaze. "That would *so* suck." To be with D all the time and not get the loving? No way.

D purred for him, hand stroking his hip.

"You turn me on -- that sound. It... I can't explain it, but it's so good."

D purred some more. "I'm going to remember that, Pet."

Then they were at the door to the ballroom, D knocking. "I'd hate to just walk in if he wasn't perfectly ready."

He nodded, leaned against D's chest with a happy sigh. The purring rumbles shook D's chest.

Wetthers opened the door, giving them a warm smile. "Happy New Year, sirs." Then the man flung the door open, revealing the room to be lit by a revolving disco ball, a rock ballad playing in the background.

"I hope it works for you, Master Matthew -- I had rather short notice."

D growled. "I didn't know before tonight either, Wetthers."

The old man winked at Matthew. "There's champagne and hors d'ouvres at the buffet table. Ring if you need me."

Matt just blinked, wide-eyed and open-mouthed. Oh. Oh, wow.

"I... D... Wow... Wetthers, just... Wow."

D grinned. "I believe the arrangements are satis-factory, Wetthers. You've outdone yourself. As usual."

"Yeah, man. Oh, wow." He grinned at Wetthers, shook the man's hand. "Gonna get him to send you on an all-expenses paid vacation one day, you just wait."

Wetthers gave him one of those looks. "Then you'd be the miracle worker, sir."

D laughed. "Thank you, Wetthers. I'm sure we won't need you again."

"Nevertheless, Sir, I will be ready should you ring."

"Good man. Happy New Year."

"Happy New Years, Wetthers!" Matt grinned and then moved through the room, laughing as the lights spun and sparkled and made him dizzy. "Too fucking *cool*, D."

"I'm glad you like it, Pet." D looked like he really was glad, like he'd put the whole thing to-gether on his own. It was cute.

There were all sorts of snacky things spread around, little veggies and cheeses and crackers. Good stuff. "I do. Wanna dance?"

"Certainly. You'd like the music turned up, I presume? So that we can feel the bass line in our feet?"

"Oh, yeah. That would be cool. Where?" He looked around for a knob, a stereo, something.

"There should be controls for the stereo by the light switch on the main door." D went and hit a couple of buttons, the music growing much louder just as the slow ballad slid into a hard edged rock tune.

"Mmm!" Matt started dancing, swaying to the beat, hips rocking back and forth. Oh, he loved this, loved dancing, loved the feeling of the music on his skin.

"I don't know this new fangled stuff, Pet," D warned him, coming up behind him and plastering against his back, following his movements.

"Mmm... nothing to know, D. Just feel, you know?" He leaned into D's strength, ass sliding against his lover over and over. Yeah. Feel.

D rumbled. "Pet... you aren't making it easy to dance."

He could feel D hard against him, cock rubbing his ass as they moved together. The large, warm hands slid along his waist and found his belly, stroking teasingly.

"Dancing's just really long foreplay." He closed his eyes, body shifting and rolling under that touch.

"How long is really long, Pet?"

"Hmm? Oh, God, D. I used to dance for hours - - five, six hours. It was *sweet*."

D growled, the sound not entirely happy. "You keep rubbing against me and there's no way I can dance for that long."

"Shh... We'll do what we need to do, D, yeah?"

He turned and took a kiss, then backed away a little. "This is supposed to be good for both of us."

"Well, I'm having a good time so far." D gave him a grin, moving toward him, the long body finding the beat and moving with it.

"Good." They moved together, sliding and then moving away, bodies brushing close and then easing apart. It was good, hot.

D started to spend more time sliding against him than away from him, and he could hear the low growls anytime D drew near. Matthew started leading the chase a little, clinging and then drawing back, letting his dragon hunt. Those fascinating eyes were glowing and he could actually smell D, smell the hunger and the want on him.

He was getting hot, sweating, and he pulled the shirt off and tossed it aside. His nipples tightened as he danced faster, staying just out of D's reach. D's nostrils flared and he copied the move, silk ripping under the hasty fingers.

Matt backed away, grabbed a piece of ice from the cooler and sucked it into his lips. "Hard work, dancing."

D growled, eyes intent, coming for him.

He kept moving, kept away from those fingers, snatching another piece of ice and rubbing it against his chest, cooling off. "Real hard work."

"Pet..."

He ran the ice around one nipple. "Yeah, D?"

D's growl was almost a roar, and then his lover leapt at him. Matt took off towards the doors like a shot, not even looking to see if the dragon was on his heels. He was, though, D grabbing him around the waist and pulling him up tight against the hot, hard body before he'd even made it halfway.

"Mine," snarled D.

The music pounded like his heartbeat, making him brave, making him want, and he met D's eyes. "Prove it."

D snarled again, eyes wild. D dropped to his knees, fingers tearing open his laces, mouth swallowing him down just like that.

"D!" His scream echoed through the room, entire body jerking violently, cock pushing deep. The lights spun furiously, making him dizzy, off-balance and his hands clutched D's shoulders, fingers squeezing.

D sucked fiercely, pulls hard and strong.

"Gonna! Oh! D! Love! Shit!" He wailed, hips snapping, so fucking close.

D growled around his prick. Matt shot hard, every muscle screaming, every nerve alive and alight. D sucked him down, every bit, tongue licking at him.

"Oh. Oh, D. D. So good. Oh." He was panting, shaking, eyes rolling as the pleasure shook him.

D's hands were hard on his hips, holding him up as D nuzzled his balls, his pubes. Oh, he was going to shake completely apart, going to die of pleasure. Going to fucking melt.

"Mine," growled D, eyes burning up at him.

"Yes. Yes, D." He nodded, head bobbing on his neck. "Yours."

D slowly nibbled and kissed up along his stomach and chest.

"We... we stopped dancing." He stroked D's temple, moaning.

D's arms wrapped around him as D nibbled at his neck, body moving against him, hard cock rubbing. "Have we?"

"Mmm... No. No, I guess not." He nestled in, licking at D's throat.

D purred for him, rubbing harder. Matthew let his hands start petting, moving in long sweeps down D's spine. It made his lover crazy, made D hard and hungry.

"Want your mouth," growled D, pushing into his touches.

"I can handle that." He went to his knees, cheek rubbing the hot hardness of D's prick through the leather. D made a noise that he would have called a whimper in another lover.

Fastening his mouth over D's balls, he exhaled hard, heating the soft skin while his fingers worked open D's fly.

D's hands slid through his curls, stroking his scalp. "Sweet Matthew, my dear Pet setting me on fire."

He repeated the action again and again. Finally he could breathe against D's skin, the leather parting for his touch. D's prick slid out, pushing toward his mouth. Licking, sucking, he teased his way to the tip, lapping and gently fucking the slit with his tongue.

"Pet... Oh. When did you get so good at that?"

He moaned, pushing a little harder, hands tracing D's belly. He had a good imagination. D's moan answered him, vibrating through D's cock, lower and more visceral than the beat vibrating up his knees through the floor. Matthew just closed his eyes, sinking into the taste and feel of D in his mouth, ass swaying to the music, hands exploring.

D's hands tightened in his hair, almost but not quite holding him in place. He started bobbing, taking as much as he could, swallowing around the tip. D moaned and growled, hands slowly tightening on his head, hips beginning to move. He forced himself to relax, to open up, to believe D wouldn't hurt him, choke him.

D fucked his mouth slowly, purrs and growls and wicked words falling down on him. It made him hard again, made him need. Made him ache. D's hips moved faster, beginning to snap a little. He could feel the prick in his mouth growing even harder.

He swallowed hard, hands holding on tight, sucking and tugging at D with his lips. Fuck, yes. More. Please. D's fingers tightened almost to the point of pain, his lover roaring, coming, shooting down his throat. Matt swallowed as much as he could, letting the rest fall onto his belly, hot and wet.

D's hands gentled, stroked through his curls. Long, rumbling purrs filled the air, competed with the music. Panting, he dropped soft kisses over D's hips, D's belly.

D purred. "Happy New Year, Pet."

"Mmm... yes. Happy New Year." He grinned up, chuckling. "You going to get me drunk on champagne and have your wicked way with me now?"

"Yes."

"Oh, cool."

D chuckled, eye happy and sated. Warm.

His dragon drew him up from the floor, bringing their mouths together. He melted into the kiss, purring, happy. Home.

Yeah, all things considered, it was a very happy New Year.

# Chapter 9

Drakon was wired.

Feeding had been particularly good the last few days and he had glutted one hunger. Now it was time to glut another.

He climbed up onto the balcony of Matt's room and slid into his Pet's room. "Matthew."

Matt muttered softly, twisting in the sheets. His Pet was tangled, cloth wrapped around the flat belly, around one leg, hiding the sweet, red curls that crowned the curved shaft. Growling he went over and pulled the sheets away, untangling until his Pet was free and naked.

Shivering, Matthew frowned, hands reaching. When they hit his skin, his Pet moaned, hummed happily, moving towards his heat. He growled, wrapping around his Pet. His.

He began to nibble the sweet flesh of Matthew's neck.

"Mmm..." Matthew snuggled in, wriggling and shifting. "Sleeping, D. Shh... Sleeping."

He growled, hungry, needing. "No sleeping. Making love."

"I was having a dream. We were on a boat." Matthew wrapped closer, humming.

"A boat?"

"Mm-hmm. You and me on a big boat."

"Doing what?" he asked, licking at Matthew's lips. Less talk, more sex. He was hungry.

"Dancing." Matt grinned, kissing him, slow and lazy. "Mmm..."

"Oh... Like this?" he asked, rolling Matthew beneath him and taking that sweet mouth.

Matthew opened to him, still dozing in and out of sleep, arms wrapping around his neck, tongue sliding against his own. He rocked against his Pet, sucking on Matthew's tongue. A soft cry sounded, Matthew's eyes opening, staring up at him.

He purred, nipping at Matthew's lips. "You see? Dreaming or awake -- we're dancing."

"Mmm... yeah. Morning." Matt moaned as his teeth caught that full bottom lip. "Toothy bastard. Be careful or I'll send you to bed without supper. Breakfast. Whatever."

"I've already eaten, Pet. Now I want you."

"Pushy." Matt rubbed their bodies together.

"Do you blame me, Pet?"

"Blame you?" Yellow-green eyes blinked at him.

"For being pushy. How can I resist you?"

"Oh, yeah. Skinny. Afro. Pale. *Definitely* a catch. You're a nut."

He growled. "No one insults my Pet, Pet. Not even you." He bent and bit Matthew's shoulder, pulling up a lurid mark.

"D! Ow!" Matt jerked, gasped, cock filling against his belly.

He purred and pulled up another mark just beside Matt's nipple. His Pet loved to complain, but Matthew's body always betrayed him, proved how much he loved the biting and sucking and claiming. The tight pink nipple drew to a point for his mouth, tempting him. Soft cries filled the air. He licked it, tongue teasing the tip of it and then let his teeth graze across it.

"Oh, shit! D!" Matt blinked at him, shivering. "So much."

He snapped his teeth together in the air above Matthew's nipple, a low growl coming from him. His Pet went still, muscles bunching to escape. He growled and grabbed Matthew's arms, holding them above his Pet's head as he worked another mark into Matthew's skin. Matthew struggled, fighting him, pulling against his strength. The scent of need was strong, heady, fierce. He spread Matthew's legs with his knees, settling in the cradle of his Pet's body as he worked up a mark by Matthew's other nipple.

"Marking me, D." Matthew pulled harder, heavy cock bobbing between them, the scent of need strong and rich and wild.

"Yessss," he hissed, nipping at the tiny piece of hard flesh before moving to suck up another mark by his Pet's rib.

Matthew tasted salty, bright and wanton on his tongue. His. His Pet. The thin body twisted, moving away from his mouth.

He growled. "I should tie you down."

"You wouldn't!" Matthew's eyes were wide, blinking. His poor clueless Pet.

"I would, Pet." He transferred Matthew's wrists to one hand and let the other slide down to cup the hot balls. "I'm sure Wetthers could find me some leather bindings."

Matthew's hips went still. "No! Don't you call Wetthers in here!" Matthew *looked* at him. "You don't have him buy sex stuff do you?"

He just looked back, pretty sure the truth would not make Matthew happy.

"D! That's really gross. Really. Really, really."

He raised an eyebrow. "It's not like he tries them out first, Pet."

"Eeeeeew!" Matthew wrinkled his nose and shook his head. "That's it. No sex toys unless we order them off the 'net or we go get them."

"You can buy them off the 'net?"

Matt nodded. "You can buy anything off the 'net, D. Some shit I can't even figure out how to use."

"Oh, we're definitely getting that, then. Wait a minute." He gave Matthew a close look. "You've been looking at sex toys on the 'net?"

"Uh..." Green eyes flashed up at him. "Are you going to eat me if I say yes?"

"Of course not! Well, not in the crunchy sense, though I might in the sexual sense." He grinned down at his Pet. "What were you looking at? What did you want to try?"

"Try?" Matt shook his head. "I was just looking for leather pants. Do you *know* what comes up if you search for leather? Scary."

"Leather pants." He purred, suddenly remembering what had been interrupted by this conversation. "You could wear them with the leather cuffs. Wetthers gave you a credit card, right? You know you can buy anything you see that intrigues you, yes?" He began to nip at Matthew's neck, his Pet's wrists still held firmly in his hand.

"Yeah. Yeah, he did." Matthew moaned softly, chin lifting and letting him in.

"Next time you look up leather, buy some restraints." He bit again, pulling up yet another lurid mark. His Pet's skin took to color beautifully.

"Not going to get tied up, D." Matthew's legs bent, hips rocking up against him over and over, hard shaft sliding over his belly.

"Of course not, Pet. I can see the idea repulses you." He moved his free hand down to slide along that hard, hard shaft.

"Oh..." His Pet arched, gasping, shuddering for him.

He collected the drops of pre-come from the tip of Matthew's cock and pushed his fingers between the tight ass cheeks, making the wrinkled skin around Matthew's hole slick.

"Mmm... D..." The tight little muscles rippled for him, jumped against his finger.

Keeping his hold of Matthew's hands, he reached for the lube and slicked up his fingers. He pressed them against Matthew again.

"We need a set of restraints for your arms and another set for your legs. Leather that warms as you wear it, filling the air with the smell of leather to go with the scent of your skin and your need."

"Oh..." Matthew shuddered, body taking his fingertips eagerly, dancing beneath him. "I... D..."

"Like the way that sounds -- yes, I know." He growled softly, happily.

"You... You say things and short-circuit my brain."

"But your body always knows what to say." He nuzzled and nipped at an earlobe.

"My body wants you. All the time."

"I'll tell you a secret, Pet. I want you all the time as well."

"Not... not a secret, love. Not a secret." Matthew's cheek rubbed against his, body still rocking.

He laughed with delight. Shifting again, not letting Matthew's hands go, he settled between his Pet's legs, shaft nudging where his fingers had been. Matthew's motions took him in, swallowed him in slow, steady bits. He growled, shuddering as that tight heat surrounded him.

Matthew rocked, caught between his hands and his cock, fucking that sweet body on him. Caught, and still his Pet didn't submit, didn't back away or back down, but took him as much as he took Matthew.

So sexy.

His Matthew -- so strong, so brave. All his. His Pet.

He added the force of his own pushes to each thrust.

Matthew was gasping, eyes closed, lips parted as they moved. The flat belly was sheened with sweat, red curls dark now, cock red and hard and leaking. He roared, pushing harder, soaring with his Pet.

"Oh. Oh, D... So... So much..." Matt was muttering, moaning, purring for him.

"Yes, Pet." He licked the marks on Matthew's neck, shifting, finding the angle that slid his shaft across Matthew's gland.

The wild cry was broken, needy, hungry.

"Come for me, Pet."

"D!" Matt's eyes flew open, arms tugging hard in his hand as they body rippled, squeezed him desperately.

He roared, nipping at Matthew's collarbone as he came, filling his Pet with his heat.

Matthew slowly relaxed, moaning softly, warm

and melting around him. He kissed Matthew deeply and let his Pet's wrists go with a soft growl.

"Mmm..." Matthew moaned as his Pet moved, reached for him.

He wrapped his arms around the boy's waist, curling around his Pet.

His hunger was sated.

For now.

*** 

Pizza.

He wanted pizza.

Now.

Right now.

He untangled himself from the sheets and headed towards his room and his closet.

Cheese pizza with onions and garlic.

Lots of garlic.

He was tugging on some jeans when it occurred to him that he didn't know if D liked garlic breath.

Or onion breath.

Interesting.

He padded downstairs to find the phone. Or Wetthers. Did Pizza Hut even deliver out here at... He looked at the clock. Noon?

"Good morning, sir." Wetthers gave him a smile. The old guy was polishing the silver. People still did that. Amazing.

"Hey, Wetthers. Do they deliver pizza out here?" He gave Wetthers a grin. "And if so, wanna share a pie?"

"I can make you a pizza, Master Matthew." Wetthers put down his rag. "Meat lovers style, sir?" And damned if those eyes weren't twinkling.

"Uh, ew." He shook his head. "No, I don't want to make you work. And ick, dead pig. Cheese and onions and garlic and... oooh! Olives."

Wetthers chuckled. Actually chuckled. "I can make you a pizza, Master Matthew. Cheese, onions, garlic, olives. Anything else? Peppers, mushrooms, tomatoes?"

"Oh, yeah." He nodded, almost drooling. "I'll help, if you want."

"That's quite all right, sir. It isn't any trouble."

"I just..." He grinned. "You know how sometimes you *need* a certain flavor? I woke up and thought *pizza*."

Wetthers nodded. "Yes, sir, I do know. For me it is usually marmite."

"Marmite?" He found a chair, settling in. "What's that?"

"A vegetable yeast spread, sir. Quite nice on wheat toast."

"It's vegetarian?" He shrugged, it couldn't be any weirder than tofu, yeah? "Maybe I can try it some day? Some not-pizza day?"

Wetthers chuckled. "It's a bit of an acquired taste, but I can guarantee you there is always some on hand." Like he'd ever asked for something and had Wetthers tell him it couldn't be done.

"So, do you like pizza?" He went and poured himself a glass of apple juice. "You want some?"

"I'm more likely to nibble the ingredients as I make it, sir."

"Yeah? I love raw peppers, but not onions. My tongue is too wimpy." He kept wandering, getting a banana to curb his appetite.

"I like your tongue the way it is," growled D, coming into the kitchen in his robe.

He turned bright red, lips sliding over the banana a second before he stopped himself. "Morning, D."

D purred, arms wrapping around his waist as D nibbled at his neck. "Good morning, Pet."

Matthew blushed darker, leaning into D's warmth, snuggling. "Wetthers is making me pizza."

"A pizza?"

"Yep. Onions, olives, garlic, tomatoes, mushrooms and peppers. He rocks."

D shuddered dramatically. "Plants and fungus. How delightful."

He laughed. "Oh, yeah! Cheese, too. Lots of cheese."

"I'll pass, thank you."

"I didn't offer to make *you* any, Sir," noted Wetthers with a wink at Matt.

Matt giggled, grinning over at Wetthers, then up at D. "You'll have to convince me to share a bite."

"Oh, but a bite of what, Pet?" D wagged his eyebrows and returned to nibbling his neck, this time those sharp teeth were in evidence.

"D! Be good!" Oh, God! Wetthers was *right* there. Toothy bastard.

"I'd rather be bad," murmured D.

"The pizza will be about a half hour, Sir, if you wanted to retire." That was Wetthers way of saying "go be horny somewhere I'm not cooking, please."

D purred. "Come, Pet. I'll do you on the dining room table, and then you can have your pizza in the drawing room by the fire."

"D!" He stood, pushing D out of the kitchen. "God, you're *so* bad! Wetthers was right there!"

"And I have yet to see the man blush." D let himself be pushed, right up into a wall of the hall.

"You are... I mean... I'm going to beat you. Hard." The thought made him giggle, grinning up into D's eyes.

D purred. "Promises, promises."

He popped D's hip, hard enough to make his hand tingle, then backed away.

"Mm, Pet. Again."

"D!" He was going to catch on fire, blushing so hard.

"Don't tease, Pet." D took a step forward, eyes hot.

"Tease? I wasn't... I mean I... I just... D!" He took two steps back, cock getting stiff.

He saw D's nostril's flare, knew D could smell him.

Matthew didn't look away, just took one more step and then broke for the hallway, running as fast as he could. He heard D's roar and then sound of his very own dragon chasing him.

Up or down. Up or down. Damn it, hurry. He took the banister down to the basement, figuring he could hide in the laundry room under the sheets, if nothing else. D came straight for him, just like D always did. D always seemed to know.

Matt kept going, though, only stopping when he tripped over something and went head over heels, slamming into the ground, breath knocked right out of him.

Ow.

D growled, hands warm and gentle as he was lifted up and pulled close against the strong body.

He let D hold him, resting against his lover as he caught his breath. "Oh. Ow. You caught me."

"You tripped, Pet, so it doesn't count. This might have been the time you eluded me, yes?"

Chuckling and nodding, Matthew reached up and took a kiss. "Course, we both like what happens after you pounce, D."

"We do?" D licked at his lips and kissed him, drawing him tight along the warm body. "You're right. We do."

"Mm-hmm." He pushed open D's robe, hands moving over smooth shoulders, the strong, muscled back. "We do."

D purred for him and then picked him up. "I promised to make love to you on the dining room table."

"Oh..." He wrapped around his dragon, mouth sliding along D's jaw. "Okay. Now?"

"Yes." D carried him back upstairs, nibbling on his lips.

"Good." He pushed his hands through D's hair, petting. His lips were tingling, open, aching with the tiny bites.

The dining room table was solid against his back, D leaving his ass hanging out over the bottom. His dragon's mouth took his, devouring him. He gasped, lips opening wide, body shifting on the polished wood. So hot. D was so hot. D kissed him forever, mouth ravaging his, hands moving over his body, stroking his nerves to life. Matthew was aching, body so hard he hurt, legs around D's waist. Even his pajama bottoms were itching him, rougher than D's hands.

D pulled his pajamas off, the material tearing like it always did beneath D's eager hands. Rumbling and frowning, he nipped D's bottom lip. Hard. Of course... those hands were so warm and close and... Oh...

D purred and bit back. "Do it again, Pet."

He moaned, nipping hard enough to hurt, to make D feel it. Oh, he was hard. Really hard. D growled, the sound pure pleasure.

"I want you, Matthew."

"Yes. Now, D. Please." He shifted, trying to get closer to D's cock, D's heat. D growled again, fingers pushing against him. "More. D, I need..." His body arched, pushing onto those fingers, riding them hard.

Then they disappeared and the blunt heat of D's cock replaced them, D letting him push himself onto the fat prick.

"Oh!" His body rippled, shook, everything shivering inside him. "D!"

"Yes." D thrust into him, rocking him on the table.

He slid on the varnish, moving, slipping and held onto by D's hands and his own legs. He could feel himself stretching, spread wide and needy. D's hands wrapped around his waist and pulled him into each new thrust. He grabbed his cock, started pulling in time, so hard, wanting so bad. D growled and knocked his hand away, one of D's hot hands replacing it, tugging just as hard as D was thrusting.

He jerked, shoulders lifting off the table as he cried out, needing, heat flooding him, pouring from him. D kept moving, kept filling him over and over again, sending him higher and higher. When he couldn't bear it anymore, he screamed, seed spraying over his chest and belly. D roared and thrust one last time, filling him with burning seed.

Matthew fought to catch his breath, to focus, toes curling as aftershocks moved through him. D's cock slid away, D taking soft nibbles and tastes from his neck. Relaxing, he just sort of melted there, feeling D nuzzle and nibble and taste.

D purred for him. "Now this is what the dinning room table was meant for."

His laughter echoed through the big room. "No, D. If it was, it would be softer and have hand-holds."

D chuckled, still nuzzling his neck. "I'm sure Wetthers would be happy to arrange for any modifications you might want."

"No. No, thank you. It's bad enough that he's gonna have to wipe off butt-prints..."

D threw his head back and laughed. "Speaking of Wetthers..." D picked him up off the table and put him in a chair and then took off the silk robe, draping it around his shoulders. "I believe your pizza is ready." D went and sat in the chair next to him, perfectly unconcerned with his nudity.

"You... uh... you want me to go get you a... Oh. Hi, Wetthers." He blushed dark, staring at the *really* big mark on the table. "Smells good."

"Thank you, sir." Wetthers placed the large pizza pie in front of him along with a plate and a pizza cutter. "Would you like a soda with that, Master Matthew?" Wetthers didn't bat an eye at the stench of sex in the room, or the mark on the table or at D being starkers.

"I... uh... yes, please. Thank you." God, this was *embarrassing*.

"Very good, sir."

D was grinning at him as Wetthers went. "Relax, Pet. It's *Wetthers*."

"Well, *yeah*."

Wetthers came back with his soda. "Is there anything else, sirs?"

D shook his head. "Pet?"

"No. No, thank you. It looks great." He grabbed a piece of pizza, focusing on it instead of the whole naked-sex thing.

"Very well."

D chuckled as the door closed behind Wetthers.

"Quit laughing at me, you big, naked turkey." He grinned and stuck out his tongue, before diving back into the pizza.

One of D's eyebrows went up. "You shouldn't stick that out unless you plan to use it, Pet."

"I am. Eating pizza. Yum." He grinned, finishing a piece and making a show of licking his lips.

D growled. "You should be eating. Maybe not pizza, though."

"But this is pizza made *just* for me..." God, teasing D was *fun*.

"So was I, Pet. So was I."

Oh. He grinned, blushing dark, letting one foot reach out, trace along D's calf. D purred, those fascinating eyes going hot.

"You have the prettiest eyes, you know? So different." He grinned, nibbled a little more, foot still touching.

"As long as you like them, Pet." One of D's feet slid along his leg.

That made him shiver. "What are you thinking right now?"

"That if you don't hurry up and finish that you're going to be wearing it on your ass."

Well, *that* was romantic. He arched an eyebrow. "My ass does *not* need melted cheese *or* onions, thank you."

"No, it doesn't." D leaned close, eyes hot. "It needs me."

"It's already *had* you this morning. Afternoon. Whatever."

"Had, Pet. Past tense." D grinned at him and leaned closer, licking at the corner of his mouth.

"You can't possibly get it up again. *I* can't possibly get it up again. You want some pizza?" His tease would have worked better if he hadn't been chasing D's tongue.

"Shall we make it a wager?"

"A bet?" He started to nod, then stopped. "What are we betting?"

"You don't think we can 'get it up again'. I think we can." D sat back, giving him a sly look. "What should we play for? Sexual favors? Toys?"

He tilted his head. "Toys, I guess. Like, whoever wins gets to use whatever he wants on the other one?"

"Mmmm, perfect." D stood, cock already half hard. "Do you want to finish your pizza, Pet?"

He looked down; he'd eaten about half. "No, but let me put it up, I'll want it later. And *I* have to get it up too, D. Not just you."

D laughed. "Oh, you will, Pet. You will."

"Nope. I'm sated. Satisfied. Happy. Full. Pizzaed. Caffeinated." Nervous. So going to lose this bet if he didn't get a piece of ice to help out in the kitchen. "Be right back."

"I'll meet you in the bedroom, Pet."

"'kay."

Matt took the pizza to the kitchen, thanking God Wetthers was *not* there, dropped the pizza in the fridge, grabbed a handful of ice, froze any chance of a hard-on away and headed back up to D's room.

Go him.

When he got to D's bedroom, D was lounging in the middle of the bed, eyes hot.

He grinned, trying hard not to blush, not sure what to do next. "Hey."

"Hey," murmured D, voice husky -- almost but not quite a growl. D tapped the bed next to the long body. "Come here, Pet."

"Oh, okay." He moved across the room, holding D's robe close, then snuggled in next to D. The heat felt good -- not horny-good, just good-good.

D pushed open the robe and man-handled -- or was that dragon-handled? -- it off him.

"Pet! You're cold." Warm arms went around him, D pulling him up against that hot body. His neck was nuzzled by hot lips, his back stroked by hot hands and the unbelievable heat of D's prick slid along his balls and cock.

"Mmmm..." He cuddled close, the feeling too good to avoid, the warmth and touch and kisses too sweet to ignore.

One of D's hands dropped to stroke his birth-mark, leaving familiar tingles in its wake. It occurred to Matthew that snuggling like this was probably not helping his whole no-stiffie cause, but he wasn't hard yet, just warm and comfortable and happy and so wanted. He turned his head, took a long, slow kiss. D purred into his mouth, the sound setting vibrations moving throughout his insides.

Oh...

Oh, he *liked* that. He pushed closer, deepening the kiss, eager to feel that again. D purred again, hand still stroking along his birthmark, joining up the vibrations inside him with the tingles that were spreading along his skin.

"Oh, D..." He moaned softly, hands slowing

petting D's hair, D's back. "'s good, love."

"Yes..." D murmured, arching into his touch, long body writhing against him.

It was his purr that sounded this time, his hands fascinated by his lover's body, by D's response. D broke their kiss, guided his mouth to D's neck. Yes. He gave another happy little sound, then fastened his lips around the strong pulse, sucking and pulling, marking his dragon. His.

D's growl was full of pleasure, the long legs wrapping around him and pulling him in tight against D's heat, D's need. He pulled harder, humming, hands holding D close, still.

"Pet! Yes." D growled and started rocking against him. "So hot, Pet."

He lifted his chin, whispering low. "Mine. You're mine, D." Then he bit down on the strong column of his lover's neck, leaving another mark.

D roared, hips snapping hard against him, hands tightening on him. "More, Pet! More!"

"Mine." He left another bite and another, moaning each time his teeth sank into D's flesh, aching as they slammed together, bodies sweating, sliding.

Two of D's fingers slid along his crack, slick with oil, hot with promise. His hips moved furiously, trying to get those fingers to push in deep. His teeth fastened onto D's shoulder, mouth sucking at the super-heated skin. Then suddenly they pushed inside him, D fucking him hard, fingertips nailing his gland.

Oh! It felt so good his entire body arched, head thrown back as he screamed. His balls drew up as his hips jerked spasmodically, rubbing against those fingertips, against that hand.

"Matthew!" D's fingers pulled out of his body

and they rolled, D slamming into him as his back hit the bed.

"Yes! More!" He met each motion with his own, the need showing itself in their almost-violent thrusts, the slap of skin loud, harsh.

D took him fiercely, one hand wrapping around his prick, pulling in time with each thrust. When he came, the room dimmed and all he knew was white-hot pleasure that lit him inside. D's roar shot the light inside him with colors, suffused him with shared pleasure.

Matthew floated, curled into his lover, purring softly, completely boneless with pleasure. D licked lazily at his skin, sucking up a small mark on his shoulder. His dragon's hands slid over his skin, warm and good. Humming low, Matt fastened his lips around D's nipple and pulled gently.

D made a soft noise that was mostly purr. "You aren't trying to make another wager are you, Pet?"

"Hmmm?" He rubbed his lips over the warm flesh, tongue sliding over the tip.

"The bet. I won. Though you seem intent on trying to make things rise again."

"Oh!" He lifted his face, blushing dark. "I... I forgot." Yep. *Big* dork.

D chuckled and kissed him soundly.

"My hungry Pet."

"Uh-huh." He grinned and rolled his eyes. "My hungry dragon. So what did you win, D?"

"A toy of my choice to use on you, remember?"

"Well, yeah. But what toy?"

"Well..." D's eyes twinkled wickedly. "I was thinking we'd start slow actually. A dildo or a butt plug."

His mouth opened and he blinked. "Start... A

plug? Oh... I should've used more ice."

# Chapter 10

D showered and dressed, and then went searching for his Pet.

He needed Matthew's help. Well, he could have just let Wetthers pick up what he wanted, but he had a hunch Matthew would prefer to be the one to help.

He had no doubt his Pet would blush and squirm and protest, and be so turned on that they would make love.

"Matthew? Pet?"

"Hmm?" Matthew was humming, the book of Drakon on his lap, the laptop whirring and clicking, his Pet taking notes.

"I need a favor, Pet." He crouched next to Matthew's chair, taking a nibble from the warm, salty skin.

The corners of Matt's eyes wrinkled and those yellow-green eyes sparkled at him, the book closing. "Sure, D. What do you need?"

"For you to hook up to the 'net' so we can go shopping for your dildo. Or plug. Up to you, really."

Oh, there was that blush. "I... Uh... Okay. Yeah. Okay. I can maybe do that. Uh... Want to do it on the bed so you can sit, too?"

He grinned at his Pet. "Where ever you prefer making love will do, Pet."

"Why do you think that'll happen, hmm?" Matt was bright pink, the scent of excitement sweet. "We're just looking. Shopping. Shopping's not sexy."

Matt stood and brought the computer over to the bed, settling in and patting the mattress.

Chuckling, he climbed on and sat behind Matt. His Pet settled between his legs. "Shopping for toothpaste isn't sexy, Pet. Shopping for sex toys is by definition sexy."

Oh, his Pet's laughter tasted good in the back of his throat -- sweet and light.

"Which would you prefer -- a dildo or an anal plug?" He had his own preferences, but this was Matthew's first sex toy.

"I..." Matt hid beneath his curls. "Which is better?"

He purred, mouth sliding along Matt's neck. "Well, a dildo is better if you want a second prick around. But the plug is better if you're already getting plenty of action and want to explore different possibilities."

"Considering I live with the Eveready Bun... err... dragon, I guess the plug?" Matt's skin was hot for him, sweet. "I mean, I'm so plenty of action guy."

Chuckling, he nipped at one shoulder bone through Matthew's shirt. "Plug it is. Lets see if you can find it with this magical net of yours."

"Well, sure I can. I just go here." Matthew typed and tapped. "And then put the... words in here. And, ta-da! Pick a place."

"Oh, what's that one about a dungeon?"

Matthew clicked, gasping as the image of a tasty-looking man in leather straps appeared along with quite an extensive list of toys including whips and clamps and cuffs and plugs.

He purred. "Oh, what fun." He nibbled his Pet's ear. "If you wanted to try something other than a plug..."

"D!" Matthew shivered, cuddled back against him. "You've *used* this stuff? When?"

"You know I've been around a long time, Pet. Of course, most of it didn't have fancy names and you had to make your own..." He growled softly at the memory -- more than one Pet had made their own tools of pleasure.

"You're a perv, D." Matthew clicked and looked and backed up and clicked. The images moved quickly, his Pet shifting and wiggling against him. He slid his hands down to cup Matthew through his sweats, hand sliding along the hard prick.

"Mmm..." Matt's hips pushed up, rubbing against his hand, a low moan sounding.

He nibbled on the sweet earlobe. "Pick, Pet, before we forget why we're here."

"I... how big, D? Does the shape matter?"

"It's going into you, Pet. Lets start small and fairly narrow."

Matthew nodded, clicking for a minute and then pointing to two. One was metal, shiny and sleek, the other a bit wider, but more flexible and lighter. "One of these?"

"Why not both?" He moved one hand behind his Pet to tease at the sweet crease.

"B...both?" Matt shivered, nipples hard as tiny stones under the tshirt. "I... Okay. Yeah. But... you sure?"

At his nod, his Pet started filling out forms and arranging to have them shipped. He continued to play while Matthew typed, nibbling his Pet's ear-lobe and neck, hands stroking cock and ass, making sweet shudders go through the boy.

"I... Do you put them in to get someone stretched for making love?" Matt's voice was husky, threaded through with need.

"Yes," he murmured, hands moving to slid beneath the waistband of Matthew's pants. "You can also leave them in for some time. Can you imagine it, Pet? Being filled as you eat, read your books, take your walk..."

"Oh, God..." Matthew shivered, shaking hard. The computer was closed and set aside. "They... they're bought."

He purred. "And how long before we get to play?"

"Three days. I paid for three day air."

"Eager?" he asked, thumb sliding along the tip of Matthew's prick.

"I..." Embarrassed and aroused eyes met his. "Uh-huh."

"Me, too," he murmured, pushing Matthew back onto the bed, stripping them both and covering his Pet's body with his own.

Matt stretched beneath him, lips open and hungry. Oh, yes. Most eager.

\*\*\*

They were in the library when the plug arrived. Matthew was curled up in a chair with a book and he was lying out by the chair, napping.

Wetthers came in with a box. "Mail, sirs."

His Pet's eyes went wide, and Matthew took the box, shoving it under the chair without opening it. The whispered, "thanks, Wetthers," was adorable.

Wetthers' eyebrow rose, but the man just said, "you're welcome, Master Matthew," and went back to whatever it was that Wetthers did when he wasn't specifically needed.

"Aren't you going to open it?" Drakon asked, nudging the box with his foot.

"Huh?" Matthew squeaked and jumped. "Shit, D! I thought you were asleep!"

"I didn't mean to startle you, Pet." He grinned and sat up, finger stroking Matthew's arm. A trail of goose bumps appeared after his touch, like magic. He took Matthew's hand and turned it, leaving a kiss on the delicate skin of his Pet's wrist.

"Oh..." Matt shivered, eyes hot on his lips.

He pulled the box out from under Matthew's chair and handed it over as he nibbled on each fingertip.

Matthew took it, blinking and holding the box, just watching him. "Feels so good."

"Imagine how it will feel with one of these inside you while I do it."

"In... inside... D..." Oh, the scent of arousal, of need was strong, rich, sweet and heady.

"Open it," he growled, nibbling on the pad of Matthew's thumb.

It took a bit -- and both hands -- before Matthew managed to work the box open. The plugs were there -- one metal and cold, heavy, shiny; the other larger, but more forgiving. He put one in each of Matthew's hands, wrapping the nerveless fingers around them.

"They... the metal one's heavy. It wouldn't stay

in." Matthew was looking, turning them over, stroking them. "They're both so smooth."

"Of course they are, Pet. So they don't hurt you. We'll get a not smooth one when you're an old pro at them." He winked so his Pet would know he was teasing.

Matt's chuckles were pushed into his mouth, the kiss happy and wanton, sharp and sweet at once. He grabbed hold of Matt's tongue and sucked it into his mouth, hands sliding through the wild curls. Matt scooted off the chair, sliding into his lap with the softest little cry. He purred, moving Matthew's legs so his Pet straddled him.

Arms around his neck, his Pet held on, pushing into the kisses, feeding him moany little purrs. He worked Matthew's shirt off and then his Pet's pants, tearing them to get them free of Matthew's body without having to make his Pet move.

"D... You gotta stop that..." Still, the kisses didn't stop, Matthew didn't let go, even for a second.

"Why?" he asked. Really, it was the quickest way to get rid of the pesky things.

Matthew just rolled his eyes, shook his head. "You're hopeless."

Chuckling, he wriggled out of his own clothes, tearing away his pants when they proved as hard to remove without Matthew moving as Matthew's own had.

He nibbled at Matthew's lips. "Give me the plastic one, Pet. I think you're right about the other one not staying in."

"We gonna send it back?" The plug was pressed into his hand, Matthew clinging to him, excited and nervous all at once.

"We don't need to do that -- we'll use it when

you aren't planning to be out of bed." He took the plastic and warmed it in his hand. "Need oil," he murmured.

"There's a little lube sample in the box..." Matt's cheeks went rosy.

He purred, happy they weren't going to have to move. "Clever Pet."

He reached for the box and rummaged around until he came up with the little tube of lube. There'd barely be enough. He pulled it open and sparingly slicked up his fingers before sliding one against Matthew's crease.

Matthew tightened up, jerked. Those yellow-green shone at him, glittering in the fading sun-light. "Oh, D. D, love."

He kissed Matthew, tongue pushing into his Pet's mouth and then backing off, teeth nibbling the red lips. "Just my finger, Pet. One, two, stretch first, just like when it's me, yes?"

"Yeah. Oh, yeah." Matt moaned for him, shuddering. "God, I want you."

He nodded. "Yes, Pet. But first we'll put the plug inside you." He slipped his finger into Matthew's body, the tight heat clutching at him. Matthew whimpered, hips riding his finger, hands tightening on his shoulder.

"So sexy, Pet." He slid a second finger in alongside the first, stretching his Pet for the toy.

"Mmm... make me so hot. So hard." Matthew was whispering, whimpering, sighing against his lips.

"I love how you respond to me, Pet. Make me want you so much." He found Matthew's gland, pegging it with his fingertips.

"Oh!" His Pet arched, head falling back. "D!

Love!"

He wrapped his lips around Matthew's neck, growling slightly as he kept tapping his Pet's gland. Matthew kept crying his name, shuddering, sobbing, gasping for him.

He oiled up the plug and put it where his fingers had been, teasing Matthew's hole with it. "The plug now, yes, Pet? Take it in for me."

"Yes. For you. Please, love. I need." Matthew's eyes were wild, sparkling, drunk with passion.

He pushed gently, letting Matthew's own motions pull in the plastic. The fingers on his shoulders tightened, his Pet panting softly, biting hard on that full bottom lip. He licked across Matthew's lips, nipping at the lovely flesh, teeth knocking against Matthew's, distracting as he kept pushing.

"Oh, D. Full. So full." His Pet kept moving, kept taking the plug in.

"You're doing so well, Pet. So eager and passionate. It makes me hot -- the things you do for me."

"Need you. Never..." Matthew keened, blinking up at him. "Never felt things like you've shown me."

He just purred as the plug slid home, Matthew's body closing over the base of the toy. Matthew shook, pushing up against him, cock rubbing wet and hot against his stomach.

"So hungry, my Pet."

"For you. Please, D." Matthew took his mouth in a hard, toothy kiss, fingers tangled in his hair.

He growled, hand wrapping around Matthew's shaft, thumb sliding across the wet tip. Seed sprayed over his hand, his belly. The scent of his Pet was strong and rich, heady. He raised his hand to his mouth, licking the come from his fingers. His own cock twitched.

"How does it feel, Pet?"

"Full. Full." His jaw was nuzzled, Matthew humming softly. "Mmm... D..."

"Pet. I need you." He took Matthew's hand and kissed the soft wrist again then brought his Pet's hand down to his hardness.

"Yes." Matthew took his lips again, the kisses hungry and hard, that hot hand pumping him with sure, steady strokes.

He growled, fingers teasing the plug inside Matthew's body. "Your mouth, Pet."

Gasping, Matthew nodded, sliding down, ass moving out of range of his fingers and lips dropping over his prick. He gasped at the heat, at the suction. Matthew was becoming very good at this. So hungry, his Pet, hands and mouth working together to drive him mad. He wrapped his fingers in Matthew's hair, holding onto the curls as he growled and moaned.

Carefully, gently, one hand cupped his balls, finger sliding back to ghost over his hole as Matthew's tongue flicked over his slit. He roared, body shaking as he came. His Pet swallowed him down, mouth moving slower, softer, lips gentle on his shaft.

He purred, hands petting gently. "Can you still feel it, Pet?"

"Mmm..." Matthew nodded, hips rocking slowly. "I do. Can. Whatever."

"Good. Let's go up to my room. You can sit in the chair and read to me."

Matthew tilted his head, gave him a curious look, then nodded. "Okay, D."

Then those slender fingers reached back, tracing the bottom of the plug. "I just push it out, yeah?"

"Oh no, Pet." He took Matthew's hand and kissed the wrist again. "You keep it in until later."

"Huh? Keep it in? But..." Those eyes searched his face, his Pet's sweet cock jerking.

"Yes, Pet." He grinned. "So you can feel my gift inside you while you read."

"D..." Matt gasped, shook his head. "I... I don't know..."

Standing he picked his Pet up and set Matthew on his feet. "Come now, walk there with me."

Matthew blinked up at him, goose pimples covering the thin body. "I'm going to... to... to melt."

"Mm... wonderful."

They started moving, Matthew snuggled close to his side, soft little moans turning to a whimper as they faced the stairs.

He turned to his Pet, stroking the sweet face. "Try for me, Pet?"

Matthew nuzzled his hand. "You'll kiss me at the top?"

"I will, Pet."

By the time Matthew was at the top of the stairs, the long, thin cock was full again, a fine sheen of sweat making his Pet shimmer. "My kiss, D."

He pulled Matthew near, bending to bring their lips together. Matthew's tongue pushed into his mouth, moving slowly, so soft, so sweet. He purred, hands sliding over the sweat slick skin. His Pet was yielding, hot and liquid under his touch. So responsive. So needy.

He let one hand drift over the sweet buttocks, fingers teasing the top of his Pet's crease. A little whimper pushed into his lips, Matthew pushing into his arms, away from his hand. He followed Matthew's ass, fingers just brushing the bottom of the plug

"D..." Matthew nipped his bottom lip. "Your room."

"That's right -- you were going to read to me."

"Oh, D. I can't. I can't read, not like this." Matthew started moving them down the hall. "No sitting. No reading."

"I'm sure you can, Pet." He watched the sensuous way Matthew moved, his Pet trying to work with the plug, to keep it from moving too much. "I want you to try."

"Why?" Matthew stumbled over the edge of a rug, eyes drooping at the motion.

"Because when I take you, I want you to be begging me for it."

"Not going to beg. I'll ask nicely, though." Oh, that stubborn look was most adorable.

"We'll see, Pet." He took Matthew's hand and led him to the chair by the fire.

"At least it's padded, right?" Matt gave him a grin, a wink.

He laughed. "I'm not sure that's going to make all that much difference," he noted, sliding a finger along Matthew's cock.

The hard, hot flesh jerked, bobbing up toward his hand. "Tease."

"Perhaps. Though it is both of us I am teasing." His own shaft was hard again as well and the need to throw Matthew down and replace the plug with himself was growing.

"Yeah? Maybe I should help." Matthew's hand cupped his balls, rolling gently, eyes sparkling.

He growled low in the back of his throat.
"Pet..."

Those wicked, challenging eyes met his, fingers
circling his shaft. "Hmmm?"

He growled again. So special this one. All his.
He wrapped his hand around Matthew's, guiding
his Pet's strokes.

Those yellow-green eyes never left his, hungry
and shining and drinking him in. "My D."

"Yes, Pet." He moved their hands faster and
faster, body shivering at the sensation. So good.
His Pet's touch never failed to arouse him.

"Love you." Matt leaned over, lips fastening
over one of his nipples, the suction sharp and
strong.

"Matthew!" He cried out, hips moving into the
tight tunnel of their hands, pleasure shooting from
balls to nipple and back again.

Teeth scraped over his skin, Matthew's hand
tightening against him, thumb nudging the tip of
his prick. He roared, releasing his pleasure to Matthew's touch, heat spraying from him.

Their hands were slowly brought up to his Pet's
mouth, the soft pink tongue cleaning their fingers.
Purring, he leaned in to assist, tasting himself on
Matthew's skin, tongue tangling with his Pet's.
Matthew whimpered for him, lips fastening around
his tongue, tugging. He kept purring, enjoying his
Pet's aggression. Finally, he ended the kiss.

"You were going to read to me, Matthew."

"I never said I was... In fact, I said I wasn't..."
He helped Matthew sit, his Pet settling carefully,
gingerly.

He handed over a book and settled at his Pet's
feet, gazing up at the sweet boy. Matthew fairly

shone with sweat and need. His Pet was quite beautiful like this.

"You are a mean, mean man." Matthew's fingers were trembling as the book was opened.

"Not a man," he corrected idly, intent on the sight and scent of his Pet's need. "And I'm not mean -- I just want you to get the full experience."

"D... I *am* full." Those eyes just twinkled.

He threw his head back and laughed. "Oh, Pet, you are such a delight."

Trembling fingers turned the page and Matt started reading, voice hoarse and stumbling over the words. He slid his fingertips along Matthew's thigh, the skin warm and damp and smelling of sweet need.

Matthew gasped, shaking his head. "No touching, D. Not if you want me to think."

"You don't need to think, Pet." He bent and licked the edge of Matthew's birthmark where he could see it around the boy's hip.

"Oh. D. Fuck. It's *hot*."

Goose bumps pebbled the pale skin.

"You're hot, Matthew. Make me need no matter how much I sate myself in your body."

"Never knew I could feel so much. Fuck, D. I want you."

"I know, Pet." He met Matthew's eyes, tongue working the hot skin. "Wait. It will be better if you wait."

Those thin fingers danced over his face, petting him as Matt nodded. "My D."

He nuzzled and then turned to nip at Matthew's fingertips. "Yes, Pet. Your D."

Matthew flushed dark, eyes flashing. "You'll make me come."

"Just from this? I'd like to see that." He took Matthew's hand and bit the pad of the thumb, tongue sliding behind his teeth.

The gasp was soft, almost silent, his Pet's eyes desperate, the scent of need strong. Such a fascinating thing, this sensitivity in the hands. He licked his way across the palm and then down to Matthew's wrist, tongue tracing the blue veins.

The whimper was pure need. "D. Love. Please..."

"Yes, Pet?" He bit gently, threatening to break the skin, but not doing so.

"I want you." Matt's entire body was thrumming, pouring pheromones into the air, tempting him.

"You have me, Pet." His casual words might have been more convincing if it weren't for the growl that followed them up.

Matt leaned in, cheek brushing against his as his Pet whispered, "Take me, D. Need to come. Need to feel you."

And how could he resist that?

He could not.

With a roar, he pulled Matthew onto the floor on all fours, fingers jostling the plug as he got hold of the base.

"D! D, *please*!" Matt arched like a cat, crying out.

He deliberately jostled the plug once more and then pulled it out, slamming home and setting a fast, hard pace. Every thrust was met with a scream, a shudder, that thin body rippling around his cock, milking him.

Matthew made him so hard, so hungry, took his need and made it constant, absolute. He held on tight to Matthew's hips, fingers digging into the birthmark as he rode his Pet as hard as he could. The scent of Matthew's seed bloomed, his Pet drawing up around him almost painfully.

He roared, thrusting hard. "Now Matthew!"

Matt screamed, jerking beneath him. He roared again as his seed pushed from his body into Matthew's. Matt sobbed, sinking to the floor as he gasped for breath.

The motion pulled his shaft from its sheath and he moved to the floor as well, wrapping around his Pet, purring.

His arms were filled, Matthew cuddling close, hot and liquid and sweet and his.

# Chapter 11

The music was *fabulous* -- driving and loud, slamming into him while he danced.

Dressed in leather so tight he couldn't breathe, stompy boots and a mesh shirt that left nothing to the imagination, Matt was getting his share of attention -- one guy on either side, sweating and panting, bodies moving to the beat.

D had been a real bastard, growling and snapping and unhappy, and nothing he did made it better. So he'd left D a note, called a cab and hit the clubs, dancing out his frustration, moving until all he was was a sweaty body in a crowd.

He suddenly slammed up against a hard body, someone standing in the middle of the dance floor not moving a muscle. Knee-high black boots, tight leather pants and a just as tight leather vest with nothing beneath it, long mane of hair in wild disarray around a stark, beautiful face.

D.

Those mismatched eyes bore right into him, the aristocratic nose was flaring. D looked dangerous.

"D." He didn't back away, didn't look down. He hadn't done a single thing wrong. Nothing. At all.

Honest.

"Home," growled D.

Matt frowned, shook his head -- he hadn't been drinking, smoking. Just dancing. Nothing but fucking dancing. "Come dance with me."

"Restroom, then." D grabbed his hand and began to drag him off the dance floor.

He stumbled along behind, almost falling as D hurried him. "D! Damn it! Be careful!"

D ignored his words, continuing to pull him along, pushing through the crowd like it was wheat.

They hit the restroom, the music suddenly fading. "Christ, D, you damned near tugged off my arm."

He was shoved into a stall, D's full body slamming him up against the side of it.

"I've been looking for you, Matthew. Searching from bar to bar, following your scent." The words were growled straight into his ear. "Do you know what I did to the man who smelled like you?"

He struggled to catch his breath, trying not to panic, to give into his body's natural instinct to run. "I haven't done anything but dance. I told you where I'd be."

"I ate him." D rumbled, the vibrations going up his back. "He'd danced close enough to pick up your sweat. It made me wish that he had sucked you off, I want to know what it would taste like, to eat you through another."

He shuddered, closing his eyes at the thought that *he'd* caused somebody to die tonight. "It's not going to happen. You'll just have to wonder."

The growl in his ear was low, feral, wild. D's mouth closed over the skin just below his ear, sucking and biting.

He could feel D's fingers force themselves into

the back of his pants, the leather creaking as it gave way. "Wetthers has the car in the alley. There or here. It's your choice, Matthew."

"The car." He wouldn't put these people in danger. He couldn't. "The car, D. On the way home."

The moment the words were out of his mouth, D was dragging him again, pulling him out of the bathroom, past several startled patrons and out the back door. He briefly considered just stopping, just planting his feet and screaming furiously and seeing what would happen. He didn't *do* it, but he considered it.

The car was there, as D had said. D opened the door and pushed him in, following and tearing at his clothes almost before the door closed again.

"What is your fucking *problem*, D?" He was breathless again, goose fleshed and gasping.

The blue and brown eyes glittered at him in the passing street lights, but D didn't answer him, just tore his clothes away and began to bite and lick, feeding on his sweat and blood. The leather of his pants was shredded. If he wasn't so fucking wigged out, he'd kick D's ass. Well, threaten to, anyway.

D pushed his legs apart and he could feel the burning heat of D's prick pushing against his hole. Matthew forced himself to relax, to not fight it. Fighting made D weird, when D was already way past normal weird and into eating random people in clubs weird.

D roared as that hard cock slid into him, fucking him hard. The music was pouring out of the speakers, heavy and dark, the bass almost the same as at the club. Throbbing, D's body followed it, pushing inside him with the same rhythm. It was fast and hard, and it wasn't very long before D was biting down hard on his collarbone, shooting heat deep inside him.

His stomach clenched -- he wasn't sure if it was pain or pleasure or want, or just pure instinct, but it jerked hard and he closed his eyes, surrounded by D. He could feel D's nose sliding along his skin, feel the deep breaths D was taking, scenting him.

Closing his eyes, Matt relaxed. He hadn't done anything wrong, nothing to set D off. D continued to scent him, pulling away his tattered clothes as he did so. D was finally satisfied and settled on the floor of the car, pulling him down into the strong arms, holding him close.

He kept his eyes closed, kept his mouth closed, just focused on breathing, quiet and slow and easy. Meditative, numbing, stilling him deep inside -- it kept him from screaming, from crying, from feeling the guilt that wanted to pour out.

It might have been a minute, it might have been an hour before the car rolled to a stop. "We're home," murmured Wetthers.

D just growled, hold on him tightening.

He managed to clear his throat, speak. "Come on, Drakon. Inside. We're home."

Another growl and D managed to get out of the car without losing the tight grip on him. D carried him in, going straight for the bedroom.

There was no fight, no struggle. Hell, what was there to fight about? He'd laid down with the monster and fallen in love. He'd been a fool to think he could have things go back to normal. Of course, falling for a people-eating beast wasn't the brightest move he'd ever made, really. Maybe even less intelligent than feeling Sally Jensen up under the bleachers while her football coach father ran a scrimmage.

The thought almost made him smile.

D put him down in a chair near the bed and stripped. His very own dragon then began to build a nest out of the covers before picking him back up and curling around him in the middle of the bed. Feed, fuck, sleep. D had done this once or twice before, although he'd always been home when it happened in the past.

He brought his knees up to his chest, curling in on himself, holding himself tight, and waited for D to fall asleep so he could stop fighting the tears. D brought him closer, hand over his hip, sliding over to cover his birthmark.

Moments later, feeling safe, D's breathing evened out.

The tears were hot, salty, leaving his face swollen and his head pounding. Leaving him empty, lost. Several times while he cried, D growled and pet him, still asleep.

Killed someone. He'd killed someone. He didn't even know who, which person had bumped against him in which club. He'd marked someone -- him! He didn't eat meat, hadn't for *years*, because it was cruel and yet...

He'd killed someone just as sure as he'd stabbed them.

Matthew shook his head, stomach roiling. He told himself that loving Drakon was okay because it was natural, cycle of life, food chain. He told himself that because he couldn't stop. He had been doomed from the moment Wetthers had opened the front door.

As if thinking of the man had summoned him, Wetthers appeared, setting a tray on one of the bedside tables. "I thought perhaps you could use some tea."

Wiping his eyes and his hot cheeks, Matthew nodded. "Yeah. Thanks."

Moving slowly about the room, Wetthers picked up the clothes and slowly put it to rights. Once he was done, the old man turned to him, a sympathetic look on the lined face. "Is there anything else I can get you, sir?"

"No." He lifted his chin, refusing to let the new tears fall. It was his bed; he'd lie in it. "I'll be okay."

"Very good, sir." He couldn't be sure, but he thought that was a hint of a smile on Wetthers lips. The old man left as quietly as he'd entered.

He crawled out of D's arms and sat on the edge of the bed, drinking the glass of tea down and then pouring another, gasping as the cold condensation splashed on his thighs.

His gasp brought D awake, the brown and blue eyes focusing on him immediately, the growl low and worried. "Matthew?"

"The water's cold, D, that's all. Go back to sleep." His voice was rough, but steady, and he even managed a smile.

"Join me," murmured D, hand wrapping around the top of his thigh and tugging.

He just managed to put the glass on the tray before he was back in D's arms, cradled in the curve of that strong body.

"Stay," growled D, already half asleep again.

"I'm not going anywhere. Just let me grab my book." He scooted again, reaching over the end of the bed.

"Always reading," muttered D, nibbling idly at

his neck.

"Maybe if I'd stayed home reading tonight, I wouldn't have killed someone. I didn't mean any harm. I just wanted to dance." His tears started again, leaking slowly, head falling forward to offer D more skin.

D growled a little, sounding suddenly more awake. "You couldn't have killed anyone -- I would have smelled it on you. And you may dance for me anytime, Pet."

He just nodded. He didn't know what to say, what to do. So he didn't. D settled again, purring against him like a big cat, mouth back to moving slowly over his skin. Matt cried until he didn't have any tears left, until there wasn't anything left but Drakon's touch, Drakon's tongue.

"You are mine, Matthew. No one can touch you but me."

"Why? Why did you pick me?"

D's hand slid along the birthmark. "You came to me, Matthew. You were marked for me."

"Why?" He turned, head throbbing desperately. "You could have another. You... you're a beautiful man. Why me? Why didn't you just send me away? Why did you have me stay long enough to love you?"

D growled. "You belong to me. I don't question it." The hand on his hip tightened. "It just is."

"I don't belong to anyone. People don't *belong* to other people. Not anymore. It's illegal."

"So are dragons who eat people, Pet."

He shook his head. "Don't confuse the issue with logic, D. My head hurts."

D's kissed his forehead. "My poor Pet, thinking too hard."

"Don't make fun of me, D, please." He sighed, pressed into D's arms with a sob. "I got someone *killed*, D. I was just dancing and I got someone *killed*."

"I'm not making fun of you," snapped D. "Someone would have died tonight no matter what you did. *I* needed to feed. And I did. And I shall do it again." D snarled and growled. "I *eat* people, Pet. You know that. I am not ashamed of it, nor do I regret the lives given for mine."

"Fine." He pushed out of D's arms, sliding off the bed. "I know you eat people. I *know*. Is it wrong not to want to be the way you pick your supper out? Oh, look! Here's a cute guy who made the fatal mistake of dancing with Matt tonight. He's one hell of an appetizer!" He was going to be sick or scream or something. "I'm going to swim."

"Fine," snarled D. "Go. Swim. Be careful, though. There's a man-eating dragon lurking about."

"I'm not frightened of you. I never have been." He met D's eyes steadily, unafraid. D would love him or eat him, but the threats wouldn't work. "You want to eat me? Bring it on."

"If you aren't scared of me, what's all this fuss about me eating people?"

"You are not listening to me." Matt stomped his foot, infuriated. "*Listen* to me, goddammit! I'm up-set because you ate someone because they smelled like *me*. You eat people. Fine. That's what you do. Fine. But I don't want to be involved in the choos-ing. That makes it my fault and I can't cope with that. I can't *deal* with the fact that something inno-cent like dancing with me got someone killed!" Okay, so maybe he would yell.

Drakon roared and then roared again. "You do
not tell me what to do. I will choose who I want to
eat and you will not interfere!" Drakon's eyes were
glowing.

He crumpled, inside and out, shoulders hunch-
ing. "You can't hear me, can you? Not a word."
Matt gave up the fight, if there had ever been one.
"I'm going to my room, D. Goodnight."

Drakon roared again, changing before his eyes
into the terrible dragon. For a moment he thought
that Drakon would eat him, but then the dragon
roared once more and fled out the window.

The walk to his room took forever. Almost as
long as the blistering shower to scrub every bit of
scent from his skin. Not quite as long as the burn of
whiskey chasing sleeping pills lasted in his throat.

\*\*\*

His dreams were vague, flashes of angry wars
and roaring animals interspersed with long, misty
silences. Once he imagined Wetthers' eyes, dark
and worried, lips moving without sound. Another
time he dreamt of cool water, words encouraging
him to drink, to drink deep.

Then his dreams shifted, the scent of smoke
floating over a stone wall, the sun hidden by
clouds. Purple clouds. Dark and rolling and heavy,
and there were eyes hidden behind them.

One blue, one brown.

"D." He smiled. He couldn't help it.

"Matthew." D's voice was low and wanton, the
hand that slid between his legs hot.

"Am I dreaming?" He arched into that touch,
legs parting, chin lifting up to look into the clouds.

"If you want to be," growled D, the heat of his lover's breath sliding over his skin like smoke.

"I want you." He twisted, reaching out for his lover, his dragon, his *D.*

D's mouth covered his, tongue plundering deep, teeth slicing his lips. Whimpering, he opened wide, taste of his own blood making him shudder, wake up into the darkness. D sucked on his lips, taking the blood in. One of his lover's hands was still between his legs, rubbing and pinching the sensitive skin.

He moaned and jerked, trying to pull away from the touches, trying to push into the touches. "D!"

He got a growl in reply, D's knees insistently pushing his legs apart, that hand pulling on his balls, pressing the skin behind them and moving still further back. Hot. Fuck, he was hot. Burning. He twisted, almost moving away, then drawn back. One of D's fingers slid into his body, pushing until the rest of D's hand stopped it. He moved, riding that finger instinctively, grinding against the pressure of that hand.

The kiss gentled and deepened at the same time, and another finger slid into his body alongside the first

Matthew relaxed, melted, hands tangling in D's hair, body squeezing tight around those fingers. "Love you. More, D."

D growled, the sound sliding into a purr and then back into a growl. Another finger pushed in.

Oh...

His legs parted wide, his eyes blinking. "So full... Oh, D..."

"Full of me," purred D, eyes glowing down at him.

"Mmm... yes. Full of you." He felt dazed, liquid, so wanton.

D's fingers curled, pushing and searching and
stroking across his gland.

"D! Yes! There, love! Again!" His head fell
back, body shuddering.

D growled and repeated the movements with his
fingers, moving across the gland again and again as
D began to bite and suck at his neck. His world
shattered into a million pieces. He wasn't sure if he
came, if he didn't. All he knew was pressure and
pleasure and heat and D filling him.

D's fingers disappeared, leaving him empty. Not
for long, though; D's thick prick was soon pressing
against his hole. Moaning, he nodded, opening to
his lover, taking D in. D was thick and long and oh,
so hot. Just burning inside him. One hand reached
down, pressing his stomach, holding that incredible
heat, his own skin blazing in response.

"Mine," murmured D as he started to move,
thrusting slow and easy.

"D..." He almost purred, pleasure dissolving
him.

"Right here," said D, moving harder now,
faster.

"Yes. Yours. Take me." His hand slid further,
wrapping around his cock and pulling.

D's hand knocked his away. "Mine," growled D
as he began to stroke.

"Yours." He pulled D down for a kiss, jerking
hard into the hot touch.

D's lips sealed over his, the kiss hard and deep,
matching the thrusts that took him. His hips met
each thrust, each stroke, body shuddering, flying
into those eyes, into the sky. D began to growl, low

guttural sounds that meant D was going to come soon and fill him with unbelievable heat.

He planted his feet, grinding down against that hard cock, seed spilling from him with a cry. Roaring, D thrust into him hard and fast and then came, that heat filling him so full. He let it touch him everywhere, let that heat soothe him.

D settled next to him, lips and teeth and tongue moving over his skin as the sharp nailed fingers scraped over his skin. Whimpers sounded as Matt scooted forward, face buried in the soft skin.

"My Pet," murmured D, kissing his head.

He nodded, wrapping his arms around D's waist. "My D."

D purred, licking at his lips.

He was surrounded by heat, head swimming with pure pleasure. "You still mad at me?"

D gave him a look of pure surprise. "I'm not mad at you, Matthew."

"No? Good." He took another kiss, stroking D's hair, petting softly. "My D."

The low purrs started again, D nuzzling into his touch.

He let himself float, let himself be filled with D's love. He couldn't make things right, but he could give his lover himself, his heart, his care. One of D's legs slid over his, pulling him in close, keeping him near.

Relaxing, Matt snuggled -- weird, you wouldn't think you could snuggle with a dragon, but he did.

D's rumbles grew louder, vibrating against him.

"I love you." He whispered the words into D's shoulder. "No matter what. You have my heart."

"Yes, Matthew. Mine." One of D's hands settled over his birthmark, the other pressed against his heart.

He considered asking about going dancing again, but D felt good. He felt good. Warm. Happy. Maybe he could get D to go with him, and then when D got all riled up they could just go some-where and make out and skip the whole... eating thing.

Fucking sounded a lot better than feeding the hungry dragon.

# Chapter 12

Drakon forwent feeding, opting instead to stay with his Pet.

He slept wrapped around the boy, purring and soothing each time Matthew stirred. Matthew spoke in riddles while they slept, restless and worried, calming only with his touch, his voice.

He didn't understand; he thought they were past the worries and the doubts. Matthew himself had said he had the boy's heart. Matthew was young, there should be many years together before he was again alone. Growling softly, he pulled Matthew closer to him.

His Pet snuggled immediately, body nestling into his, making a soft, sweet noise. "Mmm... D..."

His growls grew lower, turned into a purr as he began to stroke Matthew's skin. Matthew loved his purr -- had from the beginning, from the first time those men had hurt his Pet and he had brought Matt home to stay. One hand slid around his waist, holding on lightly, petting his lower back.

He let his purr grow louder, body growing tight with need, his hunger for Matthew always so easily roused. Soft lips fastened around his nipple, pulling gently.

"Pet!" He wrapped his hand around Matthew's

head, holding it at his chest.

"Mmm... shh..." Blinky, quiet eyes met his, and Matt gave him a smile, tongue sliding slow and easy over the tip of his nipple. He purred again for Matthew, hand stroking the sweet body.

Those lovely eyes closed, lips pulling harder. He slid his leg over Matthew's as he began to rock. Matthew made a soft, purring sound, body sliding against his. He went to roll over onto Matthew, but at the last minute stayed where he was, letting his Pet lead this dance.

"Love you. My D."

He purred. "Yes, Pet. Yours."

Matt nodded, licking his way up D's chest. "Yes. Mine."

He tilted his Pet's face up, bringing their lips together, tongues tangling. Matt opened to him, moving slowly in his arms, hands quiet and so easy on his skin. He wrapped his own hands around Matthew's ass and pulled him close, their shafts rubbing together, the sensations making him growl into his Pet's mouth.

"Slow and easy, D. Just let me love you." Matt's hands trailed over him, their hips moving together in slow, easy waves. Matt was trying to kill him.

"You make me hunger, Pet."

"I love you, D." Those eyes met his with a quiet surety. "You're mine now."

He smiled and nodded. If only Matthew knew. He'd belonged to the boy from the first. It had been Matthew who'd needed convincing.

Matt brought their mouths together, tongue moving in time with their hips. He purred this time, filling Matthew's mouth with his pleasure. Matt purred back, the sound sweet and aggressive at once, his Pet meeting his desire head-on.

He rolled onto his back, bringing Matthew with him, demanding his Pet's passion, that aggression and love. It belonged to him. Straddling him, his Pet threaded thin fingers through his hair, holding his head still and controlling the kiss, taking his mouth. He purred, hips bucking at the pleasure. Matt didn't back away, pushing him down with hands and hips, nipping at his lips and rocking harder.

"Yes," he growled. "More, Pet."

"Bossy." Matt pushed harder, kissing deep, shifting so that his shaft slid along his Pet's crease.

He bucked up again, hands sliding to Matthew's ass again, pushing him down so that they met with more force. Matthew bit his bottom lip, drawing blood, making him purr.

"Need you," he hissed, hands spreading Matthew's buttocks apart.

"Yours." Matthew shifted and took him in, sinking down onto his cock.

He shouted out, hips bucking, driving himself deep.

"Mmm..." Matthew rose up, ass just holding the head of his prick, teasing him.

"Matthew... " he growled, hands sliding to his Pet's hips, readying to bring Matthew back down onto his shaft.

Matt's hips shifted, eyes gleaming. "Yes, D?"

"It's not wise to tease the dragon, Pet."

"No?" Matthew shifted again. "You sure?"

He growled again, hands tightening. "Quite sure, Pet."

"No one ever called me wise, my dragon."

He roared softly, hands pulled Matthew down

onto his cock.

"Oh... Oh, again, D." Matt pulled away, leading him on a merry chase that only had one ending.

He pulled Matthew down onto his shaft again, hips pushing up into hot passage.

"Yes. D. My D." Matthew arched, dancing above him, hard and flushed and proud.

Over and over again he pulled Matthew down, watching his Pet's face, feeling the pleasure spreading between them. One long hand reached back, cupping his sacs, rolling them. He made a noise that was suspiciously whimper-like. No one else could draw it from him, no one else could make him feel this way.

"Mine." Matthew's head was thrown back, body long and pale and stretched for him.

He roared, hands scraping down Matthew's sides as he came.

His Pet's seed sprayed over his belly, hot and thick. Purring, he slid his hand through Matthew's come, bringing it to his mouth to taste.

"Sexy beast." Matthew's eyes were warm, loving him.

He purred again, hands moving to pull Matthew down against him.

Matthew settled, one hand petting his hip, cheek nestled on his shoulder.

"Are you happy, Pet?" he asked. It was important.

Those pretty eyes met his. "Not all the time, but more than I thought anyone could be, yeah. The beast can't have me, D, not yet. When I'm old and sick maybe, but not yet."

"The beast doesn't want you yet, Matthew. You are mine. My Pet. My lover. My Matthew."

Matthew nodded. "Yours, Drakon. Just like you're mine."

"Yes. Made for each other."

His hand was brought to the dark mark on Matthew's hip. "Yes, my dragon."

He purred, stroking the mark that proved his claim to Matthew and Matthew's to him.

They were indeed made one for the other. Everything else was details.

End.

*A Private Hunger*

*Sean Michael*

*A Private Hunger*

Printed in the United States
93117LV00001B/10/A